CODE 2
EVIL NEVER RESTS

ALFREDO GARCIA

Code 2
Copyright © 2024 by Alfredo Garcia

ISBN
978-1-963254-94-5 (Paperback)
978-1-963254-95-2 (eBook)
978-1-963254-93-8 (Hardcover)

In Loving Memory of my parents

Miguel and Elida Garcia

Special Thanks to:

My wife Hortencia Garcia, daughter Janette, sons Alfredo Jr., Andres and all the rest of the Garcia family for their support.

Thanks to Paramedic

Richard Stubbs Jr.

The City Of Weslaco and to the Weslaco Fire Department
City Of Weslaco 255 South Kansas Weslaco, Texas 78599

Visit website at: www.weslaco.gov

Weslaco Fire/ E.M.S. & Rescue

120 East fifth St. 2nd floor

Weslaco, Texas 78599

Visit website at: www.weslaco.gov

Saint Pius X Church

600 South Oklahoma

Weslaco, Texas 78599

Visit website at: www.stpiusweslaco.org

Table of Contents

"Hello, Mr. Rodney, this is Frank Wilson from Rio Emergency Vehicles. I was calling you back, sir, to let you know that we will meet your number. I am lacking one unit. Our production manger is going over our inventory, and I will call you back in about an hour to give you the date of delivery of all the units you requested on our contract. Please feel free to call me back at (201) 283-0143, extension 2301."

"Mike! I don't care where you find the Module Box. Just find it."

Mike replies, "Mr. Wilson, we have a module box in the yard, but it is sitting on an old wrecked vehicle chassis."

"Mike, just take it off, strip it, and remount it. Can you do that?"

"Yes, sir, but we are giving them an older module."

"Mike, is there any difference on the style of the box?"

"No, sir."

"Then strip it, redo the inside, and remount it." "But—"

"Mike, just do what I am asking you to do. This client is our biggest company. I don't want to lose their business just because we can't fulfill our end of the contract."

"Okay, sir."

"Mike, how long before we can get the units ready?"

"I need about another month."

"You have two weeks and a half, to get them ready for shipment."

"Mr. Wilson, Frank, it doesn't give me enough time to fully prep the used box."

"Mike, do what you need to do and have them ready by that time."

"Yes, sir," Mike reluctantly answers.

"Hello, Mr. Rodney, I am calling you back to let you know that we will be ready for delivery of all forty-five ambulances, in about three weeks. Delivery date of June 23, 1971."

"Well, Frank, it's good to hear. I was concerned that your company could not fulfill your commitments. I look forward to receive our units. Thank you."

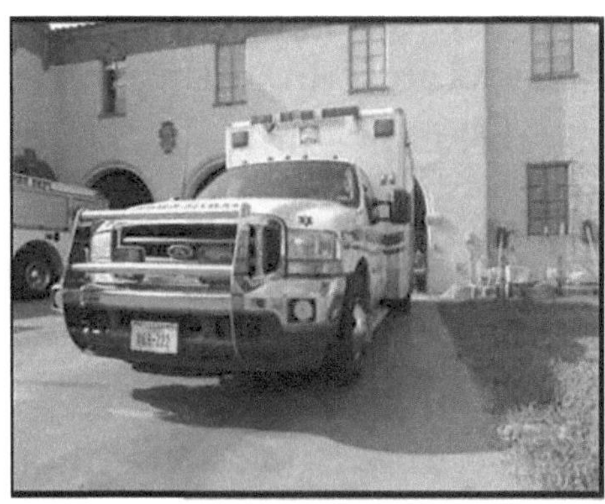

EMERGENCY CALL

It's about 10:15 p.m. when Jordan is startled and is awakened from a deep sleep. He can hear something far away. He can't make it out from where he stands, but it sounds like it's coming from the west. He runs around to the front of his house and stops, still trying to find the direction of the bothersome sound. It pierces his ears and rattles his eardrums. His body begins to shake, with anticipation, as the sound gets closer and closer. He takes a step forward; he tilts his head, confirms the sound by letting out a small bark, and begins to howl.

Far at a distance, one can hear a faint yelp from a siren. An ambulance is en route to an emergency call. The night is pitch-black. The stars shine like glitter sprinkled over a black blanket and is the only visible line, at a horizon between the earth and the sky. One can see a slight flicker of red and blue lights. They look like lights that shine on a Christmas tree.

They hide behind the branches and are only visible in certain angles.

The ambulance lights get brighter and the sound gets louder as its speeds down Barrier Lane. The lights are blinding as they pass Jordan's house. It almost seems like there was a thunderstorm, with flashing lightning bolts with an accompanying thunder of a powerful diesel engine and a whistling sound from its turbocharger.

Jordan runs and hides under his house's porch and barks at the vehicle as it streaks by the neighborhood.

Jerry Sanchez looks out the front windshield with eyes wide open. His partner is strapped to the seat with the seat belt. Jerry is a ten-year-veteran emergency medical technician paramedic and his partner, Becky Rodriguez, is a rookie basic emergency medical technician. Becky holds on with one hand on the dashboard and the other on the armrest of the door. They have been here before, but for some reason, tonight has them on edge.

Becky Rodriguez is a single mother and has just started working for the ambulance service. Her mother is her fulcrum and helps manage things in her life. She has a profound sense of loyalty to friendships and duty. She is spirited and adds a fresh point of view for her partner, Jerry Sanchez.

Jerry Sanchez is a simple young man. He loves doing what he does at his job. Like Becky, he regards friendships and a sense of duty at a high priority. He has very little time for small talk but considers himself a people person. He has a very high loyalty connection to Robert Matt, the ambulance service supervisor/director. Jerry is a very good friend to have, and the same can be said of his skill level, should one find himself or herself, in a life-threatening situation.

Tommy Reiner stands outside his patrol car, with the radio's microphone in his hand. He tries to calm down before he speaks into the microphone. Smoke fills the air. The smell of oil and antifreeze burning is suffocating. One can hear moaning and coughing by people. Children's voices are heard as they cry out for their mothers and the voices of those mothers desperately trying to reassure the children that everything will be all right. As he turns toward his left, the once quiet intersection had transformed into a chaotic junk yard, with entangled metal and broken glass scattered around the scene. He can barely make out two mangled vehicles. Two vehicles have found each other and have involved themselves in a motor vehicle collision (MVA). No, not a collision, an accident (MVA). How else would anyone assume that two separate vehicles would meet in such a tragic manner certainly not by the deliberate actions of the drivers? Why would they endanger the lives of their loved ones? One could guess it is only by accident.

Tommy communicates to his dispatcher, trying to ascertain an estimated time of arrival of the ambulance. Thumping is heard due to the failed efforts of entangled victims trying to open the vehicle doors and escape from the broken cars. The children are now screaming, their mothers desperately trying to calm them down. Tommy feels hopelessness, a situation where you want to help everyone but can't even reach a single individual.

Angrily, Tommy asks, "Dispatch, what is the ETA of EMS?"

The parents now start crying out for help. Tommy's dispatcher advises him that the best time he can get EMS is fifteen to twenty minutes. Tommy looks inside his patrol car toward the radio and screams, "What!" but then realizes that he patrols a rural area. He concedes that he and the unfortunate victims will have to settle for the ETA. He knows that they are lucky to even get an ambulance to respond. Just four years ago, there were no ambulance companies ready and able to respond. He takes a full breath of smoke-filled air, and he squeezes the microphone, asks what ambulance company is en route.

The dispatcher advises that it is Orion EMS Medic 3. Tommy feels a slight relief. He knows Jerry Sanchez and has worked with him before on several scenes. Tommy nods as if to approve and starts to approach the vehicles and assess the victims.

Tom Reiner is an assertive man. He accepts his job and understands his responsibility to the general public. He projects confidence and enjoys his job. He is the sheriff officer in charge of the crew assigned to the small rural town. The ambulance service and his department work well together. He adds a feeling of security and protection to the residents of the small town. Becky picks up the emergency radio's microphone and requests the address of the major accident.

"Dispatch, Medic 3, the location of MVA is the intersection of Farm Road 220 and Old Baggers Road."

Becky looks toward her partner, Jerry, and finds that he has turned toward her. They stare at each other for a second and appear to be puzzled. "Dispatch confirming MVA address: intersection of Farm Road 220 and Old Baggers Road. Correct?"

"Negative. Be advised address for MVA is intersection of Farm Road 230 and Old Rodgers Road. Also be advised SO (Sheriff Officer) is on scene."

"Medic 3 is clear on traffic."

"101, Medic 3."

Jerry starts to shake his head as if to say no.

Becky asks, "Do we answer him?" It is their supervisor on the radio.

Jerry grabs the microphone and proceeds to squeeze the button twice and waits. Three microphone clicks are heard. He squeezes the button once and then three more times. "101, Medic 3, 10-4."

Now Becky looks puzzled. "What was that?"

"Don't worry, I already took care of it."

Becky is lost and confused with what they did but chooses to not pursue the issue.

A phone rings in an empty room. A person awakens and drags a blanket along into the empty room. "Orion EMS, may I help you?"

A voice on the other side answers, "Hey, Bob."

Bob Matt has just been awakened and feels that he should have never come in to work. Bob is the ambulance service supervisor and director. "Jerry, what time is it?"

"It's 3:45 a.m."

"Why are calling me so early?"

"Sup, we just cleared the hospital, and we are 10-8 [back in service].We need some supplies. Can you get them for us and have them ready when we swing by the office?"

"Jerry, I'm not getting any supplies for you."

"I am just kidding. We can get our own supplies, Sup."

In the background, one can hear Becky yell out to Jerry that they have enough supplies to handle another call.

"Why did you call me this early in the morning if you knew you had enough supplies?" Bob asks.

"Sup, I just wanted to feel like you cared enough to know that your A team is alive," Jerry answers. "Good night, Sup. Sir."

Bob hangs up the phone and turns to go back to bed. As he retires back to bed, he passes his desk. On top of the desk, you can see a cardboard box labeled Medic 3 Supplies.

Robert Matt is a seasoned paramedic. The years of service have aged him but taught him well. You leave nothing to chance, always be prepared. He wears his years of service well and has a lot of good memories of the company he directs, but he feels like he is destined for something else. Every day now seems to him as if they are a prelude to something. He waits and goes on through another shift. He feels that if it doesn't happen soon, he will grow too old to do anything about it. Like Jerry and Becky, he too regards friendship, loyalty, and a good sense of duty as good character traits of emergency medical personnel.

GOOD SUNNY MORNING

Bob wakes up to a sunny Monday morning. He grabs a towel from his bag and walks over to a small restroom. He leans over a small sink, which he has been complaining about to himself as being too small to be a sink for about eleven years already. He wonders why the owner of the service never replaced it, after countless of memos Bob has left on his desk.

Bob looks up at the mirror and looks at himself. He notices that the person appears to be upset. The area between the eyebrows has several folds. He figures his mother was right: if you leave your face in a certain expression, it will stay that way. Why did he have an angry look on his face? He begins a mental check to verify that he doesn't feel like he looks. He wasn't angry at anything, or was he? *Am I hungry? Do I have any pain?* As he asks the questions, the wrinkles grow. He realizes that it's the time spent in the job that has shaped this face. He wonders how the years crept up on him so fast.

He remembers when he worked his first twenty-four-hour shift and remembers standing in front of the same sink and mirror. It's been a very long time.

Suddenly, someone knocks on the door and yells out, "Good morning, Bob! Rise and shine!"

It's the incoming B-shift supervisor, Greg Stafford. Greg is a recently certified paramedic and acts the part. Greg runs his crew like a paramilitary squad. His family all have a military history. His father and his father before him, even his older brother, is currently enlisted. Except for him, Greg. Something might have happened that Greg chose to enter into the EMS field instead. Could it have been his flat feet? He has his crew wake up really early in the morning and has them go to bed early. He has weekly checks for pressed uniforms, shined boots and is well versed on the medical protocols. After all, that is company policy. Greg's motto is "It doesn't matter how you get them there, only that you do."

"Bob, I will be in the supply room counting the supplies used yesterday," Greg says.

Bob opens the door and stops him. "Hey, uh, Greg, can you do me a favor? Can you go to my truck and get something for me?"

"Sure, Bob, what is it?"

"I got something for you."

Greg walks outside and toward Bob's truck. Bob opens a cardboard box labeled Medic 3 Supplies and begins to put back supplies he had taken earlier that morning.

Greg stops and appears to be confused. "Hey, Bob, how can I get what you want if you haven't told me what it is I am looking for?"

"Never mind," Bob says. "I think I left it at home, but I'll tell you what, I will bring it next shift."

"Well, that will be just fine," Greg says. "I look forward to next shift."

As Bob gets in his truck, Greg stands at the front door of the small building and yells out to him, "Can I ask what it is you got for me?"

Bob yells back, "If I told you, it wouldn't be a surprise! See you later." As he leaves the parking area, he starts to laugh and asks himself, how somebody can be so dumb. The radio comes on, and he hears, "101,

100, come back!" He puts his hand on his forehead and shakes his head, as if to say no. He answers the radio, "Go ahead, 101."

The voice on the radio starts to laugh on the air. "Did I make a mistake or what?"

"Negative," Bob answers. "It was my mistake, sir. I should have said, 'Go ahead, 100.'"

"That's okay, Bob, I am sure you will learn this whole code system one day. 4-10, Bob."

Bob answers, "4-10, sir."

"Anyway, Bob, can you meet me in my office this morning?"

"4-10, sir. Can you give me till about 9:00?"

"No!" George affirms. "Just kidding, Bob. Sure."

Bob pulls over the side of the road, takes a breath of fresh air, and comes to terms with the idea that he can't go home yet. He sits in his truck and tries to figure out what George White, the owner of the service, could want with him. He is a nice guy but does not know anything about EMS.

Bob arrives at the main station and takes a moment to try to enjoy the little time he has to himself. He looks out toward the main station and remembers what it looked like before it was rebuilt and converted. The building was an old mechanics shop. The shop was busy in its younger days.

Cars were everywhere and in different stages of repair. His memory takes him back, back to the day they saw it.

"Dad, is that car black?"

As we got closer, I noticed it was in fact maroon.

"Dad, what kind of car is it?"

He was too busy staring at it to answer.

"Isn't it exactly like yours?"

I got no response.

"It's a 1968 Dodge Coronet R/T," he replies, after regaining his senses. "It runs too fast."

They were there for yet another repair to be done on their car.

"Dad, why do we have to come here over and over?"

"Bobby, settle down, son. Don't you like coming here?"

"No, because he never fixes our car right.

I thought we were going to the store and get some candy."

"We'll get there in few minutes. Let's go inside."

Bob remembers how everything inside appeared very large. At only two-and-a-half-feet tall, everything looked huge. He remembers walking into the building and how long his father's strides were, after trying to match steps with his. Wasn't it amazing that his dad could walk so fast, like the comic book hero the Flash?

My father, the Flash.

Bob smiles and focuses back to the real world. Yet he still asks why his dad never answered his question of whether his dad liked the car or not. Outside the station, two ambulances are parked and are being washed. The rest of the ambulance crews are busy doing their morning check-off sheets and are getting reports from the departing crew. As he passes by, Jerry yells out to him good morning.

Just then George White comes out of the building and meets Bob halfway in the parking lot. "I did it, Bob, I did it!'"

Bob, confused, asks, "Mr. White, what did you do?"

"I did it!"

Bob smiles and asks again, "What did you do, sir?"

"I finally went and bought a new ambulance," Mr. White answers.

Bob starts shaking his head, as if to say no. Mr. White suddenly realizes that he has made a mistake. "Now, Bob, I am the, owner and I am allowed to make these types of decisions."

"Sir, you can make these types of decisions, but I thought we had agreed that it was going to be our decision as to what type of ambulance we were going to buy and what we needed."

"I know, Bob, but I could not pass up this deal. Now, I know that in the past, I've made wrong decisions on ambulances because of budget problems, but I want to let you know that on this one, I got it right."

"That's okay, sir," Bob says. "Can I ask what type of ambulance did you buy?"

"I got something better for you," Mr. White says. "It's coming in this morning. I want you to look at it and see that I can make good decisions when it comes to buying ambulances."

They both turn toward the crews.

"Well Mr. White, if what you are telling me is correct and the ambulance is awesome, these guys deserve it," Bob says.

Jerry yells out to Becky, "What's up, partner?"

"Did you hear?" Becky says. "Mr. White just bought a new ambulance."

Jerry raises his hand and gives her a high five. Suddenly, he realizes that the last two ambulances he bought didn't turn out to be very good, and one had almost gotten them killed. He starts running toward the building.

Becky, puzzled, asks, "What's going on, partner?"

"I will tell you later." Jerry runs into the building and asks the secretary for Bob. Sandra Simpson is the service's secretary, dispatcher, bookkeeper, and marketing person, a legend in her own mind.

She was hired for her good looks and nothing else. "Well, Mr. Sanchez, I will tell you if you promise to buy me breakfast."

Jerry rolls his eyes. "Okay, Sandra, now where did Bob go?"

"He is with Mr. White, and I think they went into his office."

Jerry takes off toward the office.

Sandra yells out, "I want a bacon-and-egg taco!"

Mr. White's office door swings open. Jerry looks around, hoping to see Bob but finds the room empty. He walks to the back of the building. He finds Bob and Mr. White having a meeting.

Bob is smoking a cigarette as Jerry walks up to them. "Can we help you?"

"I was wondering if I could have a word with you," Jerry asks.

Mr. White interrupts and advises Bob that the ambulance will be there in about twenty minutes and if he could stay and check the truck out. "Well, Bob, I will leave you two guys alone. I have a meeting with the bank this morning." As he leaves, he turns to Jerry and pats him on the back. "Good job last night. The sheriff's office called me this morning to thank us for our help."

Jerry waits till Mr. White walks into the building. "I thought that you had given up smoking?"

"Did you interrupt our meeting to ask me that?" Bob asks.

"No, Bob. I wanted to talk to you about this ambulance Mr. White bought. You know what happened with the last ambulance he bought. I almost got killed with it!"

"I know, Jerry, but he is the owner of the ambulance service, and he has that right to buy whatever he wants."

"I know he does, but you told me after that incident with the last ambulance that you were going to be involved in the next purchase of any ambulance."

"Look, have I ever steered you wrong, Jerry? But if you don't like the way I run things here, you are welcome to leave."

"You know I will always follow whatever you ask me to do, and you know very well I will not work anywhere else if you are not there."

"Look, Jerry, you will always be my friend, but for now, just trust me on this one, okay?"

Jerry smiles. "You got it, Bob."

From a distance, Becky is a witness to what just happened and has just decided to further investigate what her partner and the supervisor have with each other.

"101, 102." The radio comes on.

"101, go head, this is 102."

"Could you make your way to station one, please, at the request of 100?"

"10-4, en route."

"101, traffic."

"10-4. 100 purchased a new ambulance and has asked us to give him our opinion on it."

"That's a big 10-4. 102 en route to station one."

Bob has called a meeting. A majority of the employees are in attendance. The bay area is half full with personnel. They are eager to see the new ambulance and ready to condemn it to another budget gone awry. They wait in anticipation to see if the owner will once again sacrifice safety for financial stability. If he does, it won't be a surprise. Just another day at Orion Emergency Medical Service.

"Okay, everyone," Greg says. "I kept some of you here, and I know some of you need to go home, but I needed to let you know that the administration has taken it upon itself to go and purchase a new ambulance, and it will be here in a few minutes. Please try not to condemn it really quick for the owners' sake. Try to look for the positive things that we could use, and we will take it from there.

"B-shift crew, I will ask that you evaluate the unit in a fair way, and if you have any reservations on the ambulance, please try to keep it to yourselves. If you choose to write these things down, please feel free to bring them to me. I will take those concerns and file them in our very important filing cabinet." Greg points to the trash can.

Everyone in the room lets out a large laugh and applauds him. Bob shakes his head and claps. Now everyone in the room begins to yell and laugh. Even Sandra agrees that was funny and claps.

Just then you can hear a slight rumble, and through the windows, you can see a slight glimmer of chrome as the sunlight hits it. The sun's rays are refracted off the diamond plate in multiple directions, like spotlights and it pierces the windowpanes. The rumble follows the side of the building toward the parking area. The sound makes the walls vibrate just a little but lets you know it is not a small ambulance. The diesel engine is steady as it stations in the parking lot, and a slight whistle is heard as the engine winds down and idles.

Everyone stops laughing.

Becky yells out, "It's here!"

No one moves. They look at each other and wait to see who will have the courage to start walking out to see the new ambulance.

"I can't believe this. Okay, guys, the ambulance is here. Is anyone going outside?" Bob asks.

No one moves.

Greg then stands up and says, "If no one is going outside, then we are going to swipe and mop the inside of the entire station."

Jerry adds, "The reason we don't move is because we haven't gotten an order to do so, for you, Greg, sir."

Everyone laughs and start to run outside. Greg had to break the ice. The ambulance is parked in middle of the parking lot. The sun is shining on the front bumper as well as on every diamond plate on the unit. You can barely make out what is attached to the bumper from the glimmer off the aluminum diamond plate and chrome. The bumper extends forward from the chassis. A chromed push bar holds two siren speakers along with two red and blue LED emergency lights. From the glare, you could barely see that the emergency lights were on. On top of the extension, two large air horns are positioned pointing toward either side of the ambulance. The cab was clean—tented windows, spotlights, LED emergency lights all around. It was every medic's dream of an ambulance. The ambulance was painted mostly white, with reflective vinyl lines and lettering.

Red, white, and blue was the overall theme applied to the ambulance. It almost looked like the American flag. Everyone was busy checking every contraption and every compartment. The ambulance appeared to meet everyone's expectation, except for Bob's. He looks toward an arriving vehicle. George White has arrived and is all smiles.

"How much did you pay for this unit?" Bob asks.

George replies just as someone turns the siren on. He asks George to meet with him in his office. As they walked to the building, they pass Becky, who is admiring the ambulance from a distance. She over hears Mr. White telling Bob that once Bob knows how much he paid for the unit, Bob will be surprised. She stands there, wondering why the owner of this service would answer to the supervisor, an employee.

The door to Mr. White's office swings open.

"George, how much did you pay for the ambulance?" Bob asks.

"Look, Bob, I really think that you are going to be surprised."

"Look, George, that ambulance looks like an eighty-to-ninety-thousand-dollar ambulance. Don't tell me you spent that much for it! If you did, where did you get the money? You have employees that need their payroll checks! George, how could you do something like that?"

George just looks at Bob and smiles. "You won't believe how much I paid for it. I paid ten grand for it."

Bob stands, surprised. "What? Ten thousand dollars!"

"Here is the bill of sale."

Bob looks at it and smiles. "I guess you really did it, George."

"I told you, Bob. I can make good decisions."

"Did he have any more?"

George replies, "No. Not that I saw there at the lot."

"Let's go over there to see if he can get some more ambulances in the same condition."

They both get in Bob's truck and take off to the car lot.

While driving George Mentions that the car lot is on Farm rd, 220.

"George, there is no Farm Road 220," Bob replies.

"Of course there is," George answers. "I was there this Friday afternoon. I had gone over there to see some land I wanted to buy. Sure, I got lost for a little bit, but I remember the road sign."

"Can you get there again?"

George replies, "Sure!"

THE CAR LOT

After about an hour of driving, George starts to get nervous. Bob realizes that George is lost and can't remember how to get the car lot. "Hey, George, don't tell me you're lost."

"No, I am not lost," George says. "Keep driving, it's a little further."

Suddenly, something jumps in front of the truck. Bob swerves to avoid from hitting whatever it was and ends up in a small ditch.

George starts to scream. "We are going to die! We are going to die!"

"Hey, we are not going to die, we are stopped!"

They both get off the truck and look at the front tire. The tire is flat. Bob radios in that he needs help with a new tire. Greg responds to assist. While they wait for help, George wanders off across a small thicket to pee. They find themselves in a desolate area. They are surrounded by tall grass and short trees.

If it wasn't for the road that cuts through the grass, you would never know it was there. Bob finds it strange that there are no birds singing. Everything is eerily still, except for a very slight breeze that's blowing. The street appears dry, almost gray. He wonders why it is called blacktop. Why not graytop? By the condition of the asphalt, it hasn't carried any vehicle in quite awhile. The directional lines appear faded and cracked. The broken dividing line has all but disappeared. The boundary lines are pale yellow, as the asphalt slowly swallows them and turns them into grayish black. The shoulders are gone and buried under the thick tall grass. The grass appears like golden wheat slowly swaying with the wind.

There's nothing beautiful about this scene. Bob knows the grass is dying or almost dead. They haven't seen much rain this season. Being the son of a farmer, he remembers the desperate efforts his dad would try to get water to their crops, only to have them die a few days later. The sun is shining bright yet appears green through his sunglasses and slightly bites at his exposes skin on his neck. It's weird, but he remembers the days at the farm as being exactly like today.

"I found it," George says. "The car lot, I found it. Hey, Bob, come over here!"

Bob runs over, and now they both are standing in front of an old weathered building. Judging by the font, it might be from the mid-seventies.

The front of the building has large glass windows, dingy of course, but are intact. Grass and vines have grown all over the exterior walls, except for the large windows and the front door. The exterior paint is weathered and cracked.

They wipe away the surface dust and grime off the glass and try to look inside. The office area has a single desk. The drawers are sagging, and the countertop is full of buildup dust over a small pile of papers— probably fliers or applications for credit forms. As they look around, they notice that they are in the car lot parking area. The poles are erect but are pitted with rust, all except for one, which has fallen over and lost its battle to the rust. Ropes with red and white canvas flags dangle from some of the rusty poles. Grass has pushed its way through the asphalt and stand as if to claim victory as it basks in the midday sun.

Bob asks George if he is sure this was the place where he bought the ambulance.

"Yes," George answers. "I remember the small building, the flags, and the poles, but they were new. The building was new, the pavement was new."

"Do you remember the name of the place?"

"No, but the bill of sale does have the name."

Bob walks over to the truck and brings the receipt. The receipt appears to be aged and dusty. The name of the place is faded, the paper looks old, but they can make some letters out: Baggers Road Cars—the best in the county.

From a distance, they can hear people yelling their names. As they make their way toward the truck, Bob comes across an old plywood sign. It reads, Baggers Road Cars—the best in the county.

It's Greg and his crew. "Hey, guys, we are here." They replace the tire and return back to town.

They pull in the station. The off-going crew has already left, and the new ambulance is still in the parking lot. Greg starts the unit, moves it forward, and begins to drive into the station's bay. He tries to brake. He immediately deploys the emergency brake. The truck suddenly stops and rocks back and forth.

Bob runs over. "What happened?"

"I don't know," Greg answers. "I tried braking, and the brake pedal went all the way to the floor."

"Okay, Greg, don't let anybody drive this truck," Bob says. "And have Larry the mechanic check the brakes. Ask him to go through all the truck before we try putting it into service."

"Yes, sir."

As Bob is driving home, he notices that George has left the bill of sale for the new ambulance in his truck. Already too far from the station, he decides to call the main station.

"Orion EMS, this is Sandra, may I help you?"

"Hey, Sandra, it's Bob Matt. Can you let Mr. White know that he left the bill of sale for the new ambulance in my truck and I will be at the station tomorrow morning to drop it off?"

"Sure, Robert. Excuse me, can I ask you something?"

"Sure, Sandra."

"I know that I haven't worked here long and I haven't had a chance to meet everyone yet, but I was thinking; would you be interested in having dinner with me? Any day of the week or weekend, whenever it's okay with you."

Bob smiles. "Sandra, are you asking me out on a date?"

"Well, if that is what you want call it," Sandra says. "I guess Friday would be the best time for me."

"Well, Friday it is then," Bob says. "I will be looking forward to it. Bye."

Bob decides to visit and check up on his parents. He pulls up to his parents' house. The house somehow makes him feel warm when he visits. While he sits in his truck staring at the house, his mother opens the screen door and yells to him, "Yes, this is the Matt residence, and you are welcome anytime."

For a moment, Bob feels like a young thirteen-year-old boy getting home from football practice. He has a feeling like you can't wait to sink in to the home-cooked meal because you're hungry as hell. As you get closer, you can almost smell that home-cooked meal. He walks over to his mother and gently kisses her on the cheek. At that moment, all is forgiven and a feeling of warmth fills both of them. "Love you, Mom."

"Love you more," she replies. "I thought I smelled something familiar: manwich sandwiches!"

"Hey, where's Dad?"

"You know your father," Bob's mother replies. "I've called him four times already, and he has not stopped working."

Bob smiles and walks outside toward the garage. He can hear tools falling and an angry voice cursing the car being worked on. He walks over and finds his dad under the car, trying to grab a tool entrenched in some out-of-reach place in the car's engine compartment. "God help me! I don't know why anybody would build an engine compartment so small that you can barely fit an engine it."

"Hey, Dad," Bob says.

"Oh, you scared me, son! I didn't hear you come in."
"I know. You were too busy cursing the car you love."

His dad smiles. "You heard that?"

"Yes, all the way inside the house."

"Well, your mother is going to be mad at me for that."

Bob laughs. "Women. You can't live with them, and you can't live without them. I learned that from you. Hey, food's ready. Mom wants you to stop working already and wash up for dinner."

"Well, I don't care what your mother wants, I am busy."

"Hey, Dad, it's manwish night."

"Oh, never mind, got to wash up. Hey, Bobby, I'll race you.

They both run into the house.

After dinner, Bob tries to help with the dishes.

"Son, go talk with your father," Bob's mother says. "I can clean the dishes myself. I'm not that old yet."

Bob walks outside and finds his dad sitting on an old rocking chair. "Hey, Dad, what's up? I didn't want to scare you like I did earlier."

"What's troubling you, son?"

"What makes you think I have some troubles?"

"I saw it on your face since we were in the garage."

"Man, I can't hide anything from you guys, can I?"

"No, just like the time you tried to steal a candy from Old Man Troy's store. I can still see your face, scared and face as white as a ghost when Old Man Troy was talking to you."

"Okay, if I had a penny for every time I heard that story."

They both start to laugh. After a while, Bob asks his father about the old car lot. "Hey, Dad, was there an old car lot called Baggers Road Cars in this county?"

His dad becomes eerily quiet. "Where did you hear that name?"

"Well, me and the boss were out over by Farm Road 230 and got lost for a bit, and I ended up getting a flat tire."

"Was anyone hurt?"

"No. I wasn't going too fast. Anyway, I radioed in for some help. While we were waiting, the boss had to urinate. He wandered off into some thicket and found an old car lot." Bob tries to hide any emotions as he tells the story. "We looked around for a while, and we found some information about the car lot. The name was Baggers Road Cars."

His father leans over. "Bobby, stop looking up information on the car lot. You have to leave it alone. I want you to swear to me that you will stop digging into this car lot."

"Hold on, Dad, I am just asking. There is no need to get upset. I am sorry I brought it up."

"Now, your mother is coming. This conversation stops now."

"Wow, do I have that much power to silence two grown men?" Bob's mother says. "You two better not be arguing. You two know I am always right. Isn't that right, honey?"

"Yes, honey, you're right," Bob's father says. "Now, if you don't mind, son, I am going inside to watch TV, and I don't want to be there by myself for too long."

"Yes, dear."

"Okay, guys, good night," Bob says. "I haven't made it to my apartment since I got off shift this morning." He gets in his truck and drives off.

His dad stands by the front door as he drives away.

OLD FRIENDS

That same morning, Becky bumps into Jerry at the station. "Hey, partner, what are you doing here?"

"Hey, Becky," Jerry says. "I came to drop off the spare keys to the supply room. I took them early this morning. You?"

"I'm just here to pick up a copy of a payroll history report for the food stamp office. Hey, I wanted to talk to you, if you have a little time?"

"Sure."

"So what is going on here, Jerry? I am really confused and lost."

"There is nothing going on. What are you talking about?"

"I am talking with you because I am considering a job with Quincy EMS," Becky says. "It seems like this whole operation is upside down. I need to know that if there is a problem at any call, someone has my back and is looking out for me."

"Look, Becky, I have been with this company for almost eight years, and right now, this company is the most stable."

"What do you consider stable? All I see are secret messages, owners that don't behave like owners, and my own partner doesn't give me straight answers. I don't consider this as being stable."

"Well, Becky, you can do anything you want. I don't want you here if you don't want to be here. I just want to say that you are a good medic, and I would hate to see you leave. Now, as far as Bob and I, we have a good history together. I don't like to talk about that, but I guess you're not going to take no for an answer. I guess working together for so long, something is bound to stick to you. I remember many calls where we both were left dumbfounded because of things people do to each other and to themselves. We have seen the most awful things, but we still love the field."

Jerry goes on speaking. "I remember a call once where we were called out to an apartment complex for a complaint of bleeding to the private area. The normal thing to think is, 'What a poor pregnant woman.' I wonder what PARA or GRAVIDA is she. We arrive at the location, and we were directed to the second floor of the complex. I remember that we both looked at each other, thinking, 'How are we going to lower the patient down? I hope this patient is small in size and lightweight. I hope she can walk down the stairs. I hope she can speak English.' I have another story about that very issue, and I will tell you all about it later.

"Anyway, we asked all those question in that split second when we looked at each other. You know, that look you give each other when you're about to lift the stretcher. That second before you lift, when you look toward your partner and both of you sync together. That is exactly what we did. We reached the apartment, and we walk in, ready to see a woman with her legs open and crowning. What do we see? A half-naked man with his legs spread open and bleeding from his 1 percent [penis]. I remember Bob turning to me and saying, 'This call is yours, I am the lead medic, and this is a basic call.'

"How quickly lines are drawn. Well, I had to suck it up. After taking the patient to the hospital, we found out that this man had searched through the Internet and found a person to perform the surgery. Apparently, the patient's religion allowed him to implant an object in his penis. The whole idea behind it was to satisfy his spouse. What it entails is they must meticulously file a porcelain object into a shape of a heart. They try to insert it just below the first layer of skin, at the head of the penis. Of course, the object had to be very small. What happened? The patient couldn't stand the pain, and he moved. When he did, the gentleman doing the surgery cut a little too deep."

"Ouch!" Becky exclaims.

"That is exactly what I said. Well, the rest was history."

They both laugh.

"Look, Becky, when Bob gave me the responsibility of training you, I fought it as much as I could. I didn't want a rookie. You changed my point of view and made me a better medic. Now you want to leave!"

"Look, Jerry, right now, I have to go home and get the kids ready for school, but if you ever cause me not to trust you, I will leave. I'll see you next shift, okay, partner?"

Jerry smiles and shakes Becky's hand.

"KB1437 Orion EMS, we have a request for an ambulance for MVA [motor vehicle collision] and a complaint of a woman giving birth."

"Medic 3 to dispatch, we have two complaints at the MVA."

"10-4. Address will be at the intersection of Belton Street and Second."

"Medic 3 to dispatch, could you log us down en route?"

Frank and Joe jump into the unit and take off to the MVA. They arrive at the location, where they are met by SO Tommy Reiner. The intersection is already drawing a crowd. Tommy tries to block onlookers and ushers rubbernecks to continue driving.

Two vehicles are involved by what Frank sees. The vehicles are mangled together, and steam is pouring out of the engine compartments. You can barely make out drivers and passengers in the vehicles. The lead medic at the scene is Joe, as per company policy. Frank, being a paramedic himself, understands the policy and immediately begins to triage the scene.

Joe sizes up the scene. He looks around the area for any other threats to his scene. He radios in for possible additional units. Frank is meticulously walking to the vehicles and first assessing the number of potential patients. He categorizes each into age groups and then into life-threatening injuries. The first vehicle has four possible patients. The driver is entangled in the vehicle and is pinned to the seat with the steering wheel. He is conscious but is bleeding profusely through a laceration to his eyebrow. The laceration appears to be about five inches long and cut down to the bone. The passenger is conscious, oriented, and alert to person and place only (COA×2). She doesn't appear to have any obvious injuries. The rear-seat passengers are fine. Both are talking and appear to be minors.

The second vehicle has one patient. The driver is COA×3 and is able to exit the vehicle. No other complaints are voiced, and he is refusing to be transported to the hospital. Frank approaches Joe to give him a report of what patients they have. Frank is puzzled that he cannot find the pregnant patient in the vehicles. He radios in to dispatch. "Dispatch, do we have a description of the vehicle the pregnant patient is in?"

"Stand by, Medic 3."

Joe radios in for addition units to respond. "We are going to need the fire department's ETA and advise them that we need help to immobilize the patients. Please advise FD that we have a total of three patients on scene that we need help with, and advise them to speak to the medics on scene. We are next to our unit."

He then turns to Frank. "Frank, once we know where the pregnant patient is at, we are going to place her on high priority. Make sure that we get her triaged and into the ambulance ASAP. The first arriving ambulance is going to transport her. The second unit should take the young victims. We will transport the older stable patients."

"You got it, partner."

The scene is being managed like a well-oiled machine. "Dispatch to Medic 3, Rio Valley EMS is requesting if you need them to respond for assistance? Also for your 10-14, FD is en route, with an ETA of three minutes."

"10-4, advise Rio Valley that we need two units to respond to our location."

Becky and Jerry are caught still at the station and don't even hesitate. They jump in Medic 1 and respond. Becky garbs the radio microphone, and radio's in, "Medic 1 dispatch, log us down en route to MVA."

"10-4, Medic 1."

"Medic 1 to Medic 3."

"Go ahead, Medic 1."

"Medic 3, we should be on your scene in eight minutes. Where do you need us?"

"For your 10-14, you will be transporting the possible pregnant patient. We will advise you where to situate your unit. Please stand by. Dispatch, log down FD is on location."

"10-4, Medic 3. Also, the pregnant female is located inside the farm equipment store off of Belton Street."

Frank rushes to the store to assess the female. "205 to 203. The patient was not involved in the MVA. Patient is a gravida 4 and a para 3, and she is eight months along on her pregnancy."

"Medic 1 is 10-4 on traffic. Medic 1 to dispatch, we're on location."

"10-4, Medic 1."

"203 to 201, can you meet me by Medic 3?"

Jerry rushes over to Joe. "What's up?"

"You're the senior medic," Joe says. "Do you want to take over the scene?"

"Joe, you're doing a fine job," Jerry says. "If you need me to help you, I will be here. You're doing good, keep up the good work."

Becky immediately begins to help with the pregnant female.

Frank goes and assists the fire department personnel with the immobilizations. "Medic 3 dispatch, log down Rio Valley EMS is on location. 203 to 205, do we have any patient ready for transport?"

Joe is overwhelmed but is controlling the scene well. "601 dispatch, en route to the MVA."

"10-4, 601."

Joe begins to get nervous. The director, his boss, is on his way.

"601 to 203."

"Go ahead, 601."

"203, I am 63 to your location to help with the media. Could you advise them that I will be staging in the farm equipment store?"

"10-4, 601."

"Medic 1 to 203, are we cleared to transport?"

"10-4."

"Medic 1 dispatch, we are 56-63, code 1×1."

"10-4, medic 1."

Frank begins to assign patients to the arriving ambulances, and the media is ushered, by FD personnel, to their staging area at the store.

"I have a question, Mr. Matt. What happened to the pregnant female that was in the accident?" A member of the media blurts out a question.

"First, I want to let you know that before we give out any information about any possible victim, we are going to let their family members know first. Please try to understand why. Secondly, I am here to answer any questions you have as long as it pertains to the accident and my personnel. Let me start by letting you know that the medic in charge is Joe Pedron. He has over ten years of experience as paramedic and has handled multiple emergencies like this, and larger. I have complete confidence in his ability to manage this MVA. His badge number is 203. His partner is Frank Chavez, who is also a paramedic, has over fifteen years of experience. His badge number is 205. Currently, 205 is triaging the possible patients and number of patients. We will let you know as so as we know how many we have assessed. We currently don't know what happened to cause the accident, but when we do, the sheriff department will let you guys know. Okay, we can take some questions."

"Mr. Matt, my name is Willy Write. I work for the town's newspaper. I have an obvious question. If Mr. Chavez has the most experience, why don't you have him manage the emergency?"

"Well, our company policy allows for people to show that they are capable of performing their duties in stress full situations. Mr. Pedron has been working with us for a while already, so today was simply his turn to be in charge. So, Mr. Write, to further answer your question, this is not the first time Mr. Pedron has been in charge of an emergency while he has been employed with us. Does anyone else have another question?"

"Mr. Matt, I am Jodie Nickels with the daily news. My question is basically a two-part question: how do the codes work, along with the management of the emergency?"

"Good question," Bob says, as he props up a poster board. "Obviously, we don't have time to go in depth, but in general, the first-arriving ambulance's job is to do a scene size up, triage patients, and manage the transport of the patients with responding ambulances. Every component of the response has to be assigned to a specific set of rules. We use a system that allows any normal person only five things he can control safely in an emergency. We call it rule of five. If the first arriving personnel cannot fit the components of the emergency into the rule of five, he has to add a second level to one of the five components.

"You have to think of it as an outline, for example,"—he writes an outline— "vehicles in MVA, logistics, media, staging, hazards. If we had four vehicles involved in an accident and the emergency could not be managed safely, these vehicles would be assigned to a second level of control. Now the outline would read like this, for example…" He was still writing an outline:

*Vehicles in MVA

1. Vehicle commander

    1a. Vehicle one

    1b. Vehicle two

    1c. Vehicle three

and so on,

* Logistics
* Media
* Staging
* Hazards

"The names of those components could be different from my example and according to the specific emergency. In this emergency, Mr. Pedron felt that he could handle the emergency without adding any addition levels to the rule of five. Now, in order to be able to manage this emergency, every responding resource follows a similar policy, because it is a national standard.

"We use code to minimize air time. We want to leave the airwaves clear as much as possible, which plain language could totally occupy, and in an emergency, that is not good. For those of you that monitor our frequency—and I know you do—we have to communicate in short code words, chopped sentences and use the ten-code system. Police departments use different systems. For information on that, you would need to speak to our sheriff officer. Okay, I will have another meeting when we know more and when all the families are notified. Thank you."

"Mr. Matt, one last question please."

"Okay, last question, Mr. Write."

"Why isn't the first arriving unit transporting any patients?"

"It is not their responsibility to transport. The job of the first arriving unit or ambulance is to size up the scene, triage, and direct the responding ambulances to the patients. That is it. If they manage to handle the entire emergency without having to transport any patient, they have done a good job. That's all for right now."

<hr>

"203 to 601."

"Go ahead, 203."

"We are almost done. Do we stand by here to help SO with traffic?"

"10-4 stay in service, but FD is more practical."

"10-4."

"Medic 3 dispatch, be advised that we will remain at the scene to assist SO with traffic and we will be in service."

"10-4, Medic 3."

As Becky wraps the blood pressure cuff around the arm and prepares to vitalize the patient, she begins her normal routine. The process is like second nature to her. She remembers the first hands-on class in taking vital signs. She messed up at every juncture. She couldn't find a pulse at the radius, or she would find it and could not hear the thump of the heartbeat through her cheap stethoscope. She never had those kinds of problems after she bought the ultimate stethoscope.

The Littmann II SE. The difference between the stethoscopes was like night and day. No sound was too low. The investment was well worth it. Of course, her mother had to help her buy it. The best attribute of this masterpiece was that it was offered in pearl pink. It doesn't let Becky down again as she auscultates the fetal heartbeat.

"Ma'am, what is the name of your family doctor?" Becky asks.

"Dr. Peters."

"Do you have any medical history of any illness, or are you taking any medication for any illness currently?"

"No, not that I know of, except for my pregnancy."

"Who is your ob-gyn?"

The patient looks puzzled. "What?"

"Sorry," Becky says. "Who's the doctor that is handling your pregnancy?"

"Oh. His name is Dr. John Fredrickson."

"Ma'am, do you have any allergies that you know of?"

"No, I don't think so."

"Ma'am, you told my partner that you have three healthy babies and all were delivered at nine months?"

"Yes. But not all were delivered at nine months. Only one was born at nine months, the rest were born at seven to eight months."

"Okay, two were born at seven to eight months, right?"

"Yes, and we lost one. I didn't tell your friend because I really don't like to talk to anyone about it. It was very painful for us."

"Then help me understand," Becky asks. "This is your fifth pregnancy, and you delivered four babies?"

"Yes, but one was taken out by Caesarean section because it was dead, so I only delivered three."

"Ma'am, you were pregnant four times, right?"

"Yes."

"This pregnancy is your fifth, correct?"

"Yes."

"You currently have three babies, right?"

"Yes."

"Then you are a gravida-5 and a para-3," Becky says. "One last question that I know you're not going to like: what is your age?"

"That's okay, you can ask," the woman says. "Just keep it to yourself. Thirty-two years old."

"Thank you, ma'am."

Vitals are noted to be a blood pressure of 102/130, a pulse of ninety-eight beats per minute, and respirations at twenty-four breaths per minute. As they are en route to the hospital, the lights in the module flicker slightly. Becky is alarmed but tries to not show it. She was employed by an ambulance service in which these occurrences were a normal everyday thing. She recalls responding to an emergency and having rusted pieces of the roof falling like sprinkles on her lap and scenes where the ambulance would stop running, while on scene. One thing she knows she can do is work in the dark. She had to do a full assessment in the back of an ambulance with the module lights off because they were inoperative. She thinks to herself, *I can adopt and overcome!*

The patient feels nervous. Becky smiles and reassures her patient, "Ma'am, its' okay. Don't worry, we are almost at the hospital." She picks up a radio microphone. "Ma'am, I am going to talk with the hospital in a minute. Don't be afraid. It will only take a couple of minutes, okay?"

The patient reluctantly agrees.

"Orion EMS Medic 1 to Tray County ER."

No response, so Becky tries again. "Orion EMS Medic 1 to Tray County ER." She doesn't want to look toward the patient for fear of making the patient even more nervous.

"Tray County ER. Go ahead, Medic 1."

The weight is off Becky's shoulders. Any longer, and she feels that she was going to scream. "Be advised we are en route with a thirty-two-year-old female. Patient is pregnant at eight months along. She is a gravida-5 and a para-3. Patient has no known allergies to any type of medication She has no past medical history and is aware, COA×3 [conscious, oriented, and alert to person, place, and things]."

"10-4, Medic 1. Please place patient in triage area and standby there."

Becky sits there, puzzled. Medic 1 arrives at the hospital, and they promptly wheel the patient into the ER. The personnel stare at them as if to say, "Why did you have to come in right now?"

The charge nurse approaches. "Was there any reason you could not radio in?"

"We did. You even asked us to place the patient in to the triage area and asked us to standby there."

"I am sorry, but we did not get any radio transmission."

Jerry steps in. "We can check the radio in a minute. Is there a room for this patient?"

"Yes, place patient in trauma room A. What is the chief complaint of the patient?" Becky gives the nurse a report of what she has assessed.

The charge nurse returns to explain, "It's only temporary, while the maternity department cleans a room for her."

Patient care is transferred to the nurse in charge of the room, and Jerry walks outside to the ambulance and radios in to the ER. "Medic 1 to Tray County ER, can we have a radio check."

"Radio check, testing: 1-2-3-4-5-6, 6-5-4-3-2-1."

"10-4, you are coming in 10-2 [Loud and clear]."

"Okay, I guess our radios are working now," the ER charge nurse mentions as he hurries to an examination room after the doctor.

"Hey, Jerry, let's go."

They exit the ER and jump into the ambulance.

"What's up, partner?" Jerry asks. "You didn't even give me a chance to talk with my girlfriend."

"Sorry. I have a really bad feeling. Like something is wrong. I don't want to be here anymore."

"Okay, we left the ER already."

"That's not what I mean," Becky says. "I don't like this ambulance."

"I think you're overreacting, Becky."

"Look, you know I called in and they answered, right?"

"Yes."

"Jerry, the voice on the radio was a female's voice."

"Okay!"

"Didn't you notice that there are no female nurses on staff?"

"That's just a coincidence, Becky."

"No, Jerry, let's just get back to the station."

"Okay, partner."

Two days later:

"Good morning, partner," Jerry says.

Becky answers, "What's so good about it?" She smiles and proceeds to dress up with the uniform. The C-shift crew is just getting up. It's 6:30 a.m. The radio comes on, and Bob calls for 201.

Jerry answers, "Go ahead, 101."

"201, can you public service my cell phone, please?"

"10-4. Stand by."

Bob's cell phone rings about two minutes later.

"What's up, supe?" Jerry asks.

"Jerry, I need everyone to standby at the station while I get there, okay?"

"Yes, sir, no problem. What are we doing?"

"I'll let you know when I get there."

Jerry advises everyone to stay at the station and get ready ASAP because the supervisor is on his way and wants to meet with them. Becky pulls him aside. "What's going on, partner?"

"I don't know," Jerry answers. "I asked him, and he said that he will let us know when he gets here."

"I was hoping to go get some breakfast this morning before we got busy."

"Me too, but don't worry, I will make some time as long as you pay for breakfast."

They both laugh and wait for Bob.

"Okay, guys, good morning."

Everybody yells out, "Goood morning, sir!"

"Okay, that's enough, you clowns. As you all know, we just got a new ambulance, and as a tradition, we all draw names as to who will take the new unit out on its first call."

Victor raises a point. "Becky and Jerry already took Medic 1 out on its first trip two days ago."

Bob replies, "I know, Victor, but that trip was a fluke. They were not on duty, so it does not count, besides doesn't anyone else want a shot while on duty to take it to a call?"

Everyone starts to yell out and laugh.

"I am going to place the names for each crew leader in this hat, and Sandra will pull out the names of the crew that will not be driving the unit, okay? Sandra, if you will do us the honor."

As she walks up in front of everyone, they start to whistle and clap. Sandra acts the part. "Okay, boys and girls, who will it be? The first name that will not be driving the unit is Frank Arispe."

Everyone boos. "Sorry, Frank, you're out. The second crew that won't be driving the unit is Bob Matt. Oh, sorry, Robert. Who's left? The lucky driver will be Jerry and his partner, Becky Rodriguez."

Becky turns to Jerry with a big smile and says, "We got it, partner."

He answers, "Why do I have to be the lucky one all the time?"

Sandra replies, "Hah, what a poor baby."

Everyone starts to laugh and push Becky and Jerry around. Bob starts to walk outside the building, and Sandra follows him outside. "Hey, Robert, could you wait, please?"

"Are we still on for tomorrow?" Bob asks.

"Sure, I am looking forward to it."

"I will pick you up at 20:00 hours."

Sandra looks puzzled. "Huh?"

"Sorry, I will pick you up at about 8:00 p.m.," Bob says.

"Oh, okay."

As Bob walks away, he suddenly remembers something. "Hey, Sandra."

But Sandra has already gone inside the building. Bob runs back in to Sandra's desk. "Sandra, do we have a phone number for Greg Stafford?"

Sandra opens a metal drawer labeled Employees. She flips through several employee applications and finds Greg's application. "Here it is, and here is the phone number that we have on file for Greg."

They both look at the number, and Bob gets upset. "I can't believe it." The number listed was 9-Paramedic.

"Sandra, get ahold of Greg please, and have him call me on my cell phone."

Sandra notices that Bob is upset. "Yes, sir."

Bob storms out of the building, saying, "I can't believe this guy, he is such an idiot."

Bob's cell phone rings several minutes later and after he has left the station. It is Greg Stafford. "Hello, Greg." "Yes, Bob, you asked for me to call you?" "Yes, I did. Can I ask you a stupid question?" "What's up?" Greg asks.

"On your application, you listed a contact number as 9-Paramedic!"

"Ya. Pretty neat, huh?"

"No, Greg, it's not neat at all. What if I need to get ahold of you in an emergency? I would have to decipher what each letter in Paramedic stood for to call you!"

"No, I had no idea," Greg says.

"Greg, I am really upset right now over what you did, and this will go on your record. I am advising you that if you do not report to station one and fix that application in the next ten minutes, I am writing you up for providing misleading information on your application."

"Sorry, Bob, sir. I will go over there right now and fix it. This will not happen again, sir."

"I am headed over there, and I'll meet you there. I have another question to ask you." Bob hangs up and reroutes to station 1.

A vehicle arrives in the parking lot at station 1 at a high rate of speed. Its brakes are slammed, and the vehicle stops suddenly, but not before hitting the yellow concrete bumpers. Greg jumps out of the vehicle and runs toward the building, leaving the door to his vehicle open. Two minutes later, Bob drives up and sees the door to Greg's vehicle open. He walks over and notices that the vehicle is still on and one tire is on the yellow concrete bumper. He shakes his head as if to say no and starts walking toward the building. As he approaches, Greg steps outside and meets Bob in the parking lot. Greg is breathing fast, as if he had just ran a mile. He's as white as a ghost.

Sir, I just fixed it," Greg says.

Greg, you know better than that," Bob replies. "At least I hope so."

"Yes, sir, I wasn't thinking."

"Greg, I am going to overlook this one, but any more of this ridiculous stuff, and I will have to replace you. Do you understand?"

"Yes, sir, I understand," Greg answers.

"Oh, you left your car on."

"Oh, shit." Greg runs to his car and turns it off. Bob just shakes his head and smiles.

Greg runs back. "You had a question for me?"

"Yes," Bob says. "Did you have Larry the mechanic look at the new unit?"

"Yes, he said that everything checked out fine and the unit was good to run. I left a memo on your desk at our station. Did you get it?"

"I haven't made it to the station yet. Well then, thank very much. Oh, be careful when you back up your car, your front tire is on the concrete bumper."

Greg looks over toward his car. "I am such an idiot"

Bob takes off to station two.

"101. Dispatch."

"Go ahead."

"Log me down en route to station 2."

"10-4, sir."

Bob drives into a small parking area and parks in front of an old rundown rectangular building, about twenty by thirty feet. He sits in his truck and looks at the building. He remembers when the building was the center of the ambulance service. Two crews used to sleep here and call the place home. To the right of the building stands an old oak tree. The tree provided shade for several parties, which were hosted at this old station. The tree still provides shade, but for some reason, everything underneath it looks gloomy.

Bob walks into the station. The inside smells like home. He enters. To his left and at the far end of the room sits a small TV with some buttons missing. He smiles because he remembers when each of the buttons was broken off and by whom. The tube reflects the empty room as a black square with square lit panels, one panel on two of the walls. The area of the room, close to him, sits a recliner. The recliner looks about a thousand years old, but there is no other recliner like it sold anywhere. To the left of the recliner is a small folding table. It's wobbly, and faded ash stain covers the weathered wood. It has blackish-green spots where mold tried to embed itself under the varnish when some idiot forgot to bring it in after a wild night. It stayed outside through four days in the rain, held twenty boxes of pizza during Super Bowl parties, and two cases of beer during Jerry Sanchez's birthday party.

Straight ahead is a small room with a closed door. On the door hangs a sign that says Enter at Your Own Risk.

Bullet-hole stickers are all over it, and the door handle appears to have been in the Vietnam War and has done two tours. Right at the center of the door is the true identity of the room. The room that everyone has and will visit three to four times a day. The sign reads Restroom.

Far over to the right is a desk. The desk was a donation by the local school district long ago but is stout as ever. Run reports are piled neatly in a corner, ready to be reviewed. Bob rolls his eyes and tells himself, "For a minute there, I thought I was home."

MEDIC 1'S VOYAGE

"Hey, partner, let's take out the unit," Becky says.

Jerry shakes his head no. She walks over to Jerry, who is busy shining his boots. "Partner, what good is it that we won if we don't take it out?"

Jerry smiles. "Look, partner, the way I see it is I won, not you, and right now, I am busy. Besides, I have to look good driving the unit."

"Jerry, I understand where you come from, but do you think the dumbass that just crashed his car into a light pole—trapped in his mangled vehicle, barely breathing, bleeding internally, and is about to die—is going to give a shit if your boots are shiny!" Becky starts laughing and starts to wrestle Jerry to the floor.

Jerry defends himself by tickling her till she yells uncle. She then blinks her eyes at Jerry. "Can you take me to the store in your brand-new ambulance, Mr. EMS Man, pretty please?"

Jerry answers, "Okay, you idiot, let's go. But we are coming right back."

"No problem, partner."

They both walk outside and get into Medic 1. Becky turns to Jerry and says, "Let's roll, partner."

Jerry shakes his head as if to say no. "Hey, Becky, did I ever tell you the story of the funniest night Bob and I had? Back when we only had one station?"

"Yes, that's when the guy cut his penis, right?"

"No, that wasn't the funniest!"

"Then you didn't," Becky says.

"Then let me tell you the story," Jerry says, as he begins. "We hadn't received any calls all day. I remember telling Bob that we were going to be busy later that night. We decided to go to sleep early for that reason. Just in case we got busy. Just as I closed my eyes, the city police department called that they had a prisoner that needed to get checked out. You have to remember that we used to cover the city of Willsboro's contract for ambulance service. We got up and took off. It's about 9:45 p.m. Bob tells me that if we hurry up enough, we can come back to bed early. We had no idea what was in store for us the rest of the night.

"We arrived at the location, and a PD officer was waiting for us. We knew each other. He gave us a brief history, and we went inside to assess the prisoner. The cells weren't very clean. The brown paint used to paint the concrete floor and walls had chipped off. Large areas didn't have paint at all. I remember telling the jailer something about it, and he just grinned, as if to say, 'Why are you telling me for? Some people just don't get it.'

"Anyway, I was a paramedic already, and Bob couldn't dump the call on me anymore, but it was my turn to take the call. I should have known something was up when Bob volunteered to take the call. The prisoner was complaining of pain to his nose. We assessed the area, and it appeared to be fine. We asked the officer what he wanted to do, and he advised us that the prisoner could wait. An hour and a half later, the officer signed our refusal forms, and we cleared the scene. I started to make fun of the fact that I didn't have a report to write when we are called back to the police department.

"We return to the scene, and again, the officer explains that the patient is in a situation. I should have taken the first call. We walk in, and whamo! It hits us. The smell! The prisoner develops diarrhea and has an accident. Bob begins to say something, and I stopped him. I know it's my call! The poor patient had tried to sit on the toilet. Just as he went, he slipped on the diarrhea and fell on the floor.

"When he landed on the floor, it caused him to go again. He then tried to stand and slipped on the diarrhea. When he hit the floor, it caused him to go again. Poor man was lying in his own diarrhea and was slip-sliding. Like the song, 'Slip Slidin' Away.' We finally get him cleaned up and to the hospital. The smell was intense. I could still smell it on my shirt and inside the unit. Three bottles of disinfectant spray and two hours later, we cleared the hospital. While en route back to the station, we get another call. This time it is for a MVA. We turn around on the expressway median. Remember, this is when shrubs divided the expressway.

"We arrived at the location and find that four city police cars [units], two DPS troopers, and sheriff officers are on the scene. The scene appears to be really serious. We approach the lead officer, and he tells us that no one wants to go to the hospital. As he is telling us, he is smiling. Of course it is Bob's call. I offer to take down signatures from the car we can see, since it is a refusal. I reach for our tablet, and I proceed to walk to the vehicle. I noticed that there was no other vehicle which appeared to be involved in the accident.

"I finally reach the passenger door, and I ask the patient to step out of the car, and she refuses to step out. Her voice sounds weird. I asked her about it, and she mentions that it is because of the blood. I then asked the most appropriate question: 'Are you hurt?' The passenger advises that she not hurt. The DPS officer, smiling, confirms, and I then start my normal routine for a refusal. You have to remember it is pitchblack at night. I can only make out the silhouette of the car door and the patient in the passenger side. I then decide to use my trusty old minilight. I shine the light on the door, and I notice a rough texture all along the side of the door, from the window's edge toward the back door, fanning the entire passenger side.

"The rough texture stopped just short of the front seat passenger window. I asked the lady what had happened. She explained, 'We were on our way home from a friend's house, and we noticed a large object cross in front of us. I asked my husband what it was, and he replied that he didn't know. I lowered the window to see what it was, and it was right beside us. It slammed into us, and that's when we noticed it was a cow. It was big. It dented the entire left side of our car.'

"'Suddenly, we noticed that there was blood all over the side of our car. I didn't want to see the blood. I yelled out to my husband to stop. I told him I thought he had killed it. I didn't want to step out of our car. We sat in our car for about fifteen minutes before we decided to call the police. Then you guys showed up.' Then she tells me, 'I think some blood fell in my mouth.' I was confused. I again stepped back and shined the light on the car. Bob came over, already laughing, and had a larger flashlight. That is when I noticed it was feces. It was cow feces, all over the car.

"Bob took the signatures down, and we cleared the scene. While en route to the station, Bob explained what had happened. According to the officers on scene, everything that the passenger mentioned did happen, except for the part of the blood on the car. When they hit the cow, the cow defecated on the car. What hit her and what she felt in her mouth wasn't blood. It was cow poop! Huh! We both start to laugh. I turned to Bob and mentioned that I thought it was cool. We are driving around, wasting someone else's diesel and having fun. Bob mentions that he begs to differ. 'Partner, I don't know what you have been seeing tonight, but I consider it being one shitty night!'

"That was it. We pulled over, on to the expressway median, and fell out of the unit laughing. We laughed for about twenty minutes. We got back to the station at about 4:45 a.m. and just sat there, giggling. That was the most fun I have ever had in this field.

Now every time I hear the song, I smile. I guess that stuck."

Several hours later, the ambulance arrives back at the station. Jerry is angry and is upset at Becky for making them stay out for so long. "Heck, Becky, we were supposed to come right back. I don't know why we have to spend an hour looking at clothes, and to top it all off, you didn't even buy anything. If Bob gets mad, I am telling him that it was your entire fault."

Becky is laughing all the way back. "Thank you, partner, I love you."

"No, Becky, I hate to go shopping with women. You're just like all of them."

"Duh, partner, I am a girl. I can't help it if I can sucker you in to taking me shopping every time."

"Don't even ask me next shift," Jerry says. "I am not taking you anywhere."

"Okay, partner." Becky laughs, knowing that next shift, she will make him take her again.

"101, 201."

"101. This is 201. Go ahead."

"Where were you guys?"

Jerry grabs the radio and clicks the microphone twice, stops, and then clicks it twice again. "101, clear on traffic. 101 clear."

Becky is puzzled again but decides not to pursue it.

Bob is falling asleep on the recliner at his station. A flash of headlights pass through the windowpanes. He stands up and proceeds to go to the front door. He opens the door and yells out to the vehicle that has just arrived. "If you are looking to pay any bills, please go to our main station located on Tenth and Washington."

He then hears a familiar voice. "Bob, it's me."

"George?" Bob says. "What are you doing here, George?"

"I brought some goodies." George is a little drunk.

"George, you need to go home. You've been drinking, and you might have an accident."

"Aw, you weenie, I am not drunk. I want to get drunk, but I can't find anybody to get drunk with. So I came here to get drunk with you. Here, have a beer."

"George, I am on duty. You know I can't be drinking."

"I figured you were going to say that, so I have a plan B. I brought you a brown paper bag so no one can tell you have a beer in your hand." George smiles. "Just kidding. I brought you a Gatorade."

"George, thank you, but I am not thirsty."

George slightly wobbles and then stands stiff. "Look, I brought you something, and you are going to drink with me, and that's an *orderrrrr*!"

Bob grabs the bottle of Gatorade and takes a drink.

"Now, was that so bad?" George asks.

"Actually, it was," Bob answers.

George looks at Bob with an angry face. "Not drinking with you. The Gatorade. It's watermelon flavor."

They both start to laugh.

"Bob, I really like you," George says. "You are a real nice guy. Everybody respects you. They do what you ask them to do. I wish I was more like you. That is one of the reason I came here, to let you know that without you here, this company would never survived."

"George, it is not because of me that this company survives," Bob says. "It is because we have a good bunch of people working here. They like it here, and it is our job to make it fun and exciting for them. This is a team."

George replies "And there is no *I* in team."

They both look at each other and break out into laughter.

"Bob, all kidding aside. You really are the reason why we have stayed in business. You could have made it on your own. This company would have been yours."

"George, I really appreciate you saying that, even though I know that's not true. As far as me being able to stay in business, I would have run this business to the ground. This business needed you, George."

"Well, I am glad you decided to stay on and continue to run the operation. Thanks, Bob. The money I paid you really helped your parents, and I am glad for that. The offer still stands, Bob. You can be my full partner. All you have to do is say the word."

"I know, George, but I am still not ready. When I am, you will be the first to notify. Now go home before Tommy spots you and drags you to jail."

George gets into his car and drives off. Bob quickly grabs his cell phone and dials out.

On the other side of town, a cell phone rings. Tommy is on duty and is parked at the side of the main road, shooting his radar at unsuspecting oncoming drivers. "Hey, Bob, what is going on?"

"Tom, I need a favor," Bob says. "You know George White?"

"Yes, he is the owner of Orion EMS."

"He just left my station. Could you escort him to his residence? He had some beers, and I need him to make it home."

"Bob, you know that driving under the influence is illegal," Tommy says.

"You know what, Tommy? You're right. What's illegal is illegal. Like the time you stopped me and Cathy Hope. That was illegal, and no one found out anything, right?"

"You don't have to bring that up again Bob. I will find George and I'll take him home, okay."

Jerry is bored inside the station and decides to go outside and get a breath of fresh air. He looks up at the stars and tries to connect the dots to make figures with the stars. As he looks toward Medic 1, he notices that someone is behind it. He can see something run from the back to the front of the truck. One can see feet through the undercarriage of the unit. Jerry decides to check behind the ambulance and possibly catch the individuals. He reaches the ambulance and quickly goes around the unit but finds nothing. He then notices the key is still in the ignition and the master switch has been left on. He finds it funny and grins. He turns it off and starts to walk back toward the station. He hears a noise behind him. He turns quickly and finds no one behind him. He shakes his head and starts to walk toward the building.

As Jerry walks, he starts to feel a warm sensation. He feels the little hairs on the back of his neck begin to stand. He feels like someone is looking at him. The feeling is strong, but Jerry is afraid to turn around. After about a minute, he finally decides to face his fears. There, at the back of the ambulance, stands a small girl. The girl is wearing a dingy white gown. The parkingarea light is shining behind her. You can barely see her face due to the shadow off her own body. Slowly her eyes start to glisten. Her eyes become slightly brighter, and it appears her eyes are on fire. White flames rise from her eyes. He can see that she is breathing, as vapor is slightly spewing from her nose and mouth. She shows no expression but appears to wait for him to move, like a cat waiting to pounce on his prey. Her hair, now matted, swirls into horn like shapes. Like a lioness, she sizes him up.

Jerry steps back and starts running into the building. He slams the door shut behind him.

The noise awakens Becky. "Hey, what's going on?" Jerry is sitting on the sofa, watching TV.

Becky walks over. "What's with all the noise?"

"I'm sorry," Jerry says. "I tripped over the threshold when I came in."

"People are trying to sleep here." Becky returns to her bed and falls back asleep.

Jerry sits there, shaking in fear.

Becky wakes up and goes to wake Jerry and finds his bed empty. She looks out the window but gets a blast of bright sunlight in her face. For a moment, she is blinded. She steps back to regain her focus and bumps into Jerry coming out of the restroom. She is startled.

"Good morning," Becky says and gets no reply from Jerry.

Jerry proceeds to go outside the station. It is 6:30 a.m. While Jerry is outside, Becky starts to get ready to receive the incoming crew. At about 6:50 a.m., Becky finds it strange that Jerry hasn't come back in. She walks outside and sees Jerry sitting in his car. She walks over and knocks on the window. "What's up, partner?"

"Can you take care of the oncoming crew, please?" Jerry asks.

Becky agrees. Jerry further asks, "Can you cover for me? I have to go." He starts his car and speeds away. As he turns the corner of the parking lot, she catches a glimpse of Jerry's face, and it looks like he did not sleep at all.

• • •

Bob wakes up and starts his same old routine. He is staring at the mirror when he hears the sound of rustling feet outside the restroom door. He opens the door and finds Greg Stafford with his pants already undone, holding his stomach. He barely says, "Could I borrow the restroom?" He pushes Bob out of the restroom.

The next sound you hear is of a waterfall, with rocks falling along with the water. Greg makes a sigh of relief. Bob steps back and holds his nose. The smell is terrible. "Greg, are you okay?"

"Yes, I guess I ate something bad last night."

"Woof. Man, you are sick, dude."

"I'll be okay," Greg said. "I have some Pepto in my bag."

"I don't think a bottle of Pepto is going to help you," Bob says. "Can you work today?"

"Yep, I'll be okay."

"Okay, I will see you later," Bob says.

"Later," Greg says.

As Bob leaves, he can hear Greg yelling from inside the restroom, "Oh, man. God, please help me, huh!"

Bob starts to laugh.

Becky finishes with the incoming crew.

"Hey, Becky, where's Jerry?" Frank asks.

"He had to leave early," Becky answers.

"Why, cuz he ran out of tampons?"

"No, you idiot, he uses my used ones. Anyway, he had to leave early cuz his mom fell in the kitchen.

She's okay, but you know Jerry, he won't take no for an answer.

"Hey, Becky, about the whole tampon thing, I was just kidding," Frank says.

"That's okay, Frank. Anyway, Frank?"

"Yes, Becky?"

"I left a couple of tampons for you so you won't call me in the middle of the night that you ran out," Becky says.

"Oh ya!" Frank's partner high-fives Becky and starts to laugh. Frank drops the tablet and chases her out the station. Both of them exit the station, laughing. She stops running and tries to catch her breath. "Peace, Frank."

"Okay, peace," Frank says. "Hey, Becky, how did the new truck run?"

"I don't know, we had no calls yesterday," Becky says.

"You lucky suckers."

"That's right. No calls, baby. I slept like a baby."

"Like an ugly baby, you mean."

"Whatever, Frank."

They both laugh.

Becky gets her gear bag and leaves the station. She grabs her cell phone and tries calling Jerry, but the phone call goes unanswered. She continues to finish things she has to do during the day and continues trying to get Jerry on the phone. Jerry never answers. Becky, after trying all day, becomes worried. She finally decides to call Bob.

Bob's cell phone rings. He looks at the cell phone and notices that it is Becky calling and debates whether to answer or not. Missing the dinner date with Sandra is hard to resist. If he answers and Becky is on duty, they might need help. This means he has to cancel the date with Sandra, and he has been looking forward to the dinner date all week. He takes a deep breath and decides to answer the phone. "Hello, Becky. What's up?"

"Bob, something is wrong with Jerry," Becky says. "I tried calling him all day, and he doesn't answer his phone."

"Relax, Becky. Jerry is okay. He probably left his cell phone in his house and went to party with his friends."

"Bob, you know Jerry better than me," Becky says. "You know Jerry never leaves his cell phone anywhere. He is too good of a paramedic to leave his only way of communicating with dispatch. You know very well he always answers his phone."

Bob realizes that Becky is right. Jerry once returned from a hunting trip and traveled almost a hundred miles to get his phone. "Okay, Becky, I will meet you at his apartment in about twenty minutes."

IT'S NOT REAL

Becky arrives at Jerry's apartment complex. She starts to run to Jerry's apartment. She realizes she has no idea what apartment number is Jerry's. She starts to panic. Bob arrives, and Becky screams, "I don't know what apartment number he lives in!"

Bob holds her from both shoulders and asks her to calm down. "Everything will be all right. Jerry's apartment is 211."

They both run to the staircase and reach the second floor. They frantically look for room 211. Bob finds it and begins to knock on the apartment door. "Jerry, are you in there?"

"Is there a front office?" Becky asks.

"Yes, I will go get the manager with the keys." Bob leaves.

Becky starts to bang on the door and screaming. "Jerry, are you in there? Please answer the door!"

Bob returns with the manager and master keys. The door is opened, and they start to look for Jerry. He finds Jerry in the shower, crouched into a ball. Jerry is trembling and mumbling something.

Bob approaches Jerry very slowly. "Hey, Jerry, it's Robert. Are you okay?"

Jerry continues to look straight ahead and does not acknowledge him.

"Jerry, are you okay?" Bob asks again.

Becky asks if she could try. "Hey, partner. It's me, Becky. Are you okay?"

Bob notices that Jerry is actually saying something. "Becky, can you understand what he is saying?"

She gets closer and hears him whispering, "It's not real. It's not real."

"He is repeating, 'It's not real.' What is he talking about, Bob?"

"I have no idea. Let's get him out of the shower and in to bed." Bob advises the manager that he and Becky both work for the ambulance and for the manager not to worry; Jerry will be fine.

Becky sits beside Jerry in his bed and holds him. "Jerry, please tell me what's wrong so I can help you." She starts to cry.

Bob takes a deep breath and asks her to take a break. Jerry is in a state of shock.

"Becky, what happened yesterday at the station?" Bob asks.

"Nothing," Becky answers. "We had no calls. I went to sleep early, and Jerry stayed awake watching his favorite show on TV, and that was it."

"Try to remember," Bob urges. "Was there anything that happened at all?"

"Wait, there was something," Becky says. "I was sleeping, and I heard the front door slam really hard.

I got up and asked Jerry why he was making a lot of noise. He apologized, and I went back to bed. This morning, he asked me to cover for him, and he left the station in a hurry."

"So he must have been outside the station."

"Whatever it was, it must have been outside the station."

Bob gets the radio and calls the dispatch. "101. Dispatch."

"Go ahead."

"Dispatch, call SO and ask them to meet me at station 1. Also, Dispatch, could you advise the crew at the station to lock down the entire station? While you are at it, lock down your office as well."

"101, do you want to sound a code 100 [special emergency]?"

Bob stops and thinks to himself, *If I alarm everyone, would it also alarm whatever got Jerry?* "Negative. Advise SO to come in code 2." There were no lights and no sirens. He turns to Becky. "Can you handle this?"

Becky takes a deep breath and answers, "Yes, sir, supe.

Bob leaves the complex and speeds away en route to station 1.

In a flash, the enter station is surrounded with sheriff office patrol cars. Tommy calls for Bob on the radio. "SO Unit 636, 101."

"Go ahead."

"101, we are 23 at your station. Do you have any specifics on the situation?"

"10-4. We are under the suspicion that something or someone has assaulted one of our medics last night, and we are concerned that it might still be outside the station. Also, be advised I will be at your 20 in about two minutes. Gentlemen, be careful. We will start with two teams. Team 1 will start the search at the south side of the building, and team 2 will start at the north side of the building. We will meet in the middle."

Bob arrives and joins Tommy. "Tom."

"We are about to begin the search. Do you have an idea what we are looking for?"

"No, but I have a feeling we will know once we find it."

They meticulously search the entire grounds of the station and find nothing.

"Bob, we haven't seen anything."

"Keep looking we have to find it."

They search for about another hour and find nothing. "Bob, we're going to have to stop the search," Tommy says. "We have been here for three hours and a half, and we haven't found or seen anything."

"That's fine, Tom," Bob says. "Thank your guys for me."

"What happened?"

"Jerry is at his apartment with Becky, and Jerry is in shock. He saw something, or something attacked him. He is in a state of shock. He keeps repeating, 'It's not real.'"

"Look, Bob, I will have my guys do extra patrols in the area for tonight," Tommy says. "And tell your guys to call us if they see anything weird or suspicious."

"Thanks, Tom."

"No problem."

Bob's cell phone is ringing. It's Sandra. "Hey, Robert, what's going on? PD dispatcher called me that SO was there at the station with guns drawn and searching for something."

"Sandra, everything is okay," Bob says. "Jerry is with Becky at his apartment. Jerry saw something or something got to him, but he is in shock. Sandra, about our dinner date, can I get a rain check?"

"Sure, Robert," Sandra says. "Go attend to Jerry. I will see you on your next shift."

While Bob talks to Sandra, the second line is ringing. "Hey, Sandra, I have to go. I have Greg on the other line." He switches to the other line. "Hello, Greg."

"Hey, Bob," Greg says. "Sorry I couldn't go over there. I was fast asleep. I just woke up, and Frank called me to tell me what just happened. I am sorry, Bob, but I don't feel well at all. I am going to have to go home. I am calling you from inside the restroom. The Pepto hasn't helped at all."

That's okay, Greg. I will relieve you in about hour."

"Thanks, Bob."

Bob takes a deep breath and gets in his truck. He calls Becky. "Hello, Becky." She asks Bob, "Did you find anything?"

"No, nothing," Bob answers.

"Hey, can you stay with Jerry to watch him tonight? Greg just called me and asked if he could go home. He has had the runs all day."

"Way ahead of you, supe. I called my mom, and she will take the kids to school tomorrow morning."

"Good," Bob says. "I will see you in the morning, okay?"

"10-4, supe."

"Good night, Becky."

"Good night, Sup."

"Call me Bob."

STATION 2 EXPLOSION

It is 2:30 a.m. The night is filled with overactive insects. You can hear cicadas singing, hoping to attract a mate. All their song is answered by overactive crickets competing for airspace. One starts, and the other stops. Suddenly, the sound stops, and the clicking of a radio breaks the song of the cicadas.

"KB1437, Orion EMS. You have a call for a patient with a possible heart attack."

Paramedic Frank Chavez jumps up from a deep sleep, as if he was just lying there waiting for an EMS call. His partner wakes up after Frank throws a pillow at him. "Let's go, let's go!"

They both slip on their coverall uniform and slide into their boots. Frank grabs the radio. Before he squeezes the microphone, he asks his partner, "Are you ready, bud?"

His partner gives him a thumbs up. Frank squeezes the radio microphone. "Orion Medic 1 dispatch. Could we have the address of the possible heart attack, please?"

"10-4 Medic 1. Respond to Farm Road 110 and Mile 2 west."

Frank turns to his partner, and they quickly jump in the new ambulance. It starts like a match. All the LED emergency lights turn on. The ambulance comes alive. It creeps forward, and the heart of unit begins to sound. There on the front fender, just past the front door, you can read Medic 1. The sound of a siren coming out of the speakers drowns out the roar of a powerful diesel engine, and the ambulance shoots forward on its way to its destination.

Bob is already getting into his first respond vehicle. As he jumps into the driver's seat, you can hear him yelling, "No! Please no!"

The response unit takes off, making a half-moon skid in the damp ground. Rocks shoot in all directions. A single rock finds its target. It brakes through the windowpane, flies across the room, and hits a gas valve to a small space heater, which turns slightly, slowly filling the building with natural gas.

Frank Chavez is a seasoned paramedic. His partner, Joe Pedron, comes from a big city service and also has seen his share of emergency calls, but tonight, they know this is not where they wanted be. They are en route to a medic's nightmare.

"Orion Medic 1 dispatch."

"Go ahead."

"Has unit 601 responded yet?"

"601 is en route already."

"10-4. 601."

"Medic one, 601."

No one answers.

"Medic 1, 601."

No one answers.

Frank looks at his partner and squeezes the microphone. "Bob, I know you can hear me. You need to hang back. I know that every ounce of your body wants to be there, but you have to understand that you might be hindering the scene. Please, Bob, answer the radio, or can you at least tell us what is your route and current location? I don't want to come across you in an intersection."

Frank waits for a few seconds and squeezes the microphone. "Bob, come on. Answer me, please! Where are you, and what is your route?"

"SO unit 636, Orion Medic 1."

"Go ahead, 636."

"Be advised I got unit 601 on FM. 110 coming up on mile one."

"10-4."

"We are on mile 2, about a one fourth mile out from the scene."

"636. Dispatch, I will be in pursuit of one first response unit to do a possible friendly stop."

Bob is hitting the dash with his fist. He knows what he is doing is wrong, but he can't help it. If he stops, he feels that he has no love for his father, and if he continues, he has become no good to the EMS field, which he loves. He takes a deep breath and decides to speak on the radio. "601, medic 1."

"Go ahead."

"Try to maintain professional language on the radio."

"For your 10-14, I will hang back, but I will continue to the location."

"Medic 1, 10-4."

"636 is also 10-4."

Medic 1 pulls into the house. Bob's mother is frantically crying and directs the medic to the garage. Frank is the first to step into the garage. Joe follows him. They find Mr. Matt sitting down against the tire of the car he is working on. He is grabbing his chest and begins to talk to the medics.

"Hello, Mr. Matt. My name is Frank, and this is my partner, Joe. You called us because you felt pain to the chest?"

"No, I am okay."

"Mr. Matt, have you ever felt this pain before?" "No."

"Can I ask what were you doing when you felt the pain to your chest?" Frank asks.

"I was just working on this old car."

Bob's mother steps into the garage, and Joe begins to ask her questions. "Mrs. Matt, does your husband have any history of heart problems?"

She is about to answer when a different voice says, "Yes."

It's Bob.

"Bob, is your father on any type heart medication?" Joe asks.

"Yes."

"Can you get it for us, please?"

Meanwhile, Frank is already applying the heart monitor and notices that Bob has brought the stretcher. They load Mr. Matt onto the unit and begin to start an IV. Frank attempts twice and cannot get it started. Joe gets in the driver's seat and waits for his partner to advise him to clear. Bob opens the side door and enters the back of the ambulance. He notices that Frank is having trouble starting the IV. "Frank, can I try it?"

Frank whispers, "Are sure it is a good idea?"

"I am a paramedic first, and then I am a son," Bob says.

Frank signals Joe to clear the scene. Bob kneels down and holds his dad's hand. "Dad, this is going to hurt a little." He cleans the antecubital area of his father's left arm and inserts the needle. The needle breaks the skin and suddenly bends up and out of the skin. Frank looks over to the monitor and screams at Bob to clear. Mr. Matt's heart is in ventricular tachycardia (V-tach). Mr. Matt's heart is just quivering. Both Bob and Frank know that in order to stop it, they have to apply from 200 to 360 joules of electricity to the heart muscle to get it to stop.

Mr. Matt suddenly feels tightness in his chest, and Frank feels no pulse. Frank presses the shock button. In an instant, 200 joules race through Mr. Matt's body. The reaction makes his body flex and jump up. Frank asks Bob to prepare for intubation while he starts CPR. Bob just sits there still and stunned.

Frank turns to Bob and screams, "If you are not going to help, get out of my ambulance!"

Bob snaps out of it. "Sorry, partner."

"I need you to prepare for intubation, please," Frank says.

Bob opens the airway bag and opens the airway kit. He measures the tube and prepares the laryngoscope. He readies and tells his partner, "Whenever you're ready." Frank directs Bob to intubate. He inserts the laryngoscope into the patient's mouth. He pushes up on the blade, and he can see the patient's vocal chords. The area looks like two curtains slightly opened, and the opening opens further when he takes a breath. He visualizes the intubation tube passing through the vocal chords and pushes it in just past the cuff of the intubation tube. He asks Frank to confirm placement of the tube, and Frank auscultates lung sounds. He advises Bob that he is not in and asks him to remove it.

Frank, after two minutes of CPR, checks for a pulse and checks his patient's rhythm. He finds it be the same (V-tach.) He calls out to clear and presses the shock button. Now 300 joules race into Mr. Matt's body; the effect is the same. Bob moves and asks Frank to attempt to intubate. Joe yells out to his medics, "We are eight minutes out."

Frank hands Bob a bag valve mask, and Bob places it on his dad and starts to ventilate. Frank advises that he is ready and performs the procedure. He visualizes the tube going in correctly and asks Bob to check for lung sounds. He asks Frank to remove the tube. As Frank starts to remove the tube, Bob checks the tube placement again and opens his father's mouth. He notices that the tube is in correctly and connects the bag valve mask directly to the intubation tube. Frank hands Bob a CO2 detector, and Bob confirms the change of color. Frank secures the tube and asks Bob to hand him the medication to push down the tube. Bob confirms tube placement but doesn't hear lung sounds. He confirms that the lungs are rising up and down, but for some reason, there are no lung sounds in all fields.

Frank administers epinephrine down the intubation tube, and Bob ventilates the patient via a bag valve mask with supplemental oxygen at 100 percent. Frank confirms that he and Bob are clear, and presses the shock button. Now 360 joules race through Mr. Matt's body, and again, the effect makes his body jump up. Frank administers amiodarone down the intubation tube. Bob ventilates the patient via bag valve mask with supplemental oxygen at 100 percent. Suddenly, Mr. Matt awakens, and his heart rhythm returns to normal at sixty-eight beats per minute.

Joe yells out, "Do you guys want me to call it in? We're just around the corner."

"Yes, you call it in. Tell them that we are following the ventricular tachycardia algorithm and that we have administered the first dose of epinephrine and amiodarone," Frank replies.

They wheel Bob's dad into the emergency room, and they are met by the emergency nurses and ER doctor. Frank takes over and starts to give them a report. Bob is asked to wait outside, and they tell him they will notify him when they need him. Tommy arrives at the emergency room with Bob's mother.

"Bobby, how is he doing?" Bob's mother asks.

Bob looks at her with a puzzled look and answers, "He is fine."

"Bob, what happened?"

Bob leaves them there and walks outside to the ambulance loading area. He opens the back of the ambulance and stares at the inside of the ambulance. He is trying to figure out what just happened. He remembers Jerry and dials Becky's number. No one answers. Bob is telling himself, "I know I had the tube. The IV. It was in." He dials Becky's cell phone again, and she finally answers. "Hello."

"Becky, how is Jerry doing?"

"Hold on, I fell asleep on the coach." Becky walks over to the bedroom and finds that Jerry is not in bed. "He is not here. Let me check if his car is here." She runs outside to the balcony and looks down toward the parking area. His car is gone. "He must have left while I was sleeping."

"What, he is not there!" Bob exclaims.

"No. He's gone!"

Bob runs back into the emergency room. He whispers something to Tommy, and Tommy quickly steps outside and gets on the radio. Bob's mom approaches him. "Bobby, what is going on?"

"Nothing, Mom, but I am going to have to leave in a minute." He walks into his dad's room, and his dad smiles at him. The treating doctor tells Bob that all his dad's vital signs are good but the doctor might transport him to the Heart Hospital for further evaluation. Bob agrees that it's is the best thing. His mother is there with them, and she also agrees. He tells his dad that he has to leave for a bit but assures him that he will return. He kisses his dad's cheek and his mother's.

Tommy has pulled his patrol car to the ambulance area and is waiting for Bob. "Okay, Bob, where do we start looking?"

"Let's try his friend Billy Johnson's house first."

They leave the emergency room.

Jerry is driving his car and is swerving all over the road. He is crying and hitting his head. He is repeating, "It's not real, it's not real!" As he drives, you can only see the road that the headlights shine on. Suddenly, the same little girl appears in front of his car at a distance. Jerry slams on the brakes, and the car comes to a screeching stop. Jerry opens his eyes and nothing is there. He pulls at his hair and says, "Get out of my head, get out of my head!" He takes off and decides to go to station 2. He tells himself that someone there will know what to do. Jerry is unaware that no one is there.

He arrives at station 2 and jumps out of his car and runs into the building. He never notices the missing first responding unit. He opens the door and yells out, "Robert, Greg, please help me. I am going crazy!"

Jerry notices that the room is dark and turns on the light switch. In an instant, the entire building explodes in a ball of fire. Jerry is blown outside like a cannonball on fire. The building disappears. All that is left is the floor and a piece of the restroom wall. On the wall is a shattered half of the mirror Bob used to see himself every morning.

The blast creates a large flame like a mini atomic bomb. People from across town hear it. Dispatch starts to receive phone calls of people wanting to report a loud bang like a bomb. Dispatch starts to decipher the calls and finds the exact location. She covers her mouth and fumbles around with the radio microphone. A single tone is heard across all emergency responders' radios. "KB1437. To all surrounding fire departments on county frequency, we have a structure fire. Location is Mile 3 and Bitters Creek Road. Be advised it is the Orion Station number 2 that is on fire.

Within a minute, the fire departments responding are calling in that they are en route. Tommy and Bob also hear the traffic. Tommy slams on the brakes, and his vehicle starts to skid sideways. Tommy is turning his car around. The patrol car performs the maneuver easily. Tommy turns his emergency lights on and turns on his siren. "SO Unit 636. Dispatch, log me down en route.

"10-4, 636. What the heck is going on, Tommy?"

"I don't know, Chief, but I will get to the bottom of this before the night is through."

"Orion EMS Medic 2 to SO unit 636."

"Go ahead, Medic 2, this is 636."

"Sir, is 101 with you?"

"10-4."

"101, do you want us to respond to back up FD?"10-4 guys, respond."

"Orion Medic 2 dispatch, log us down en route."

"10-4, Medic 2."

Bob dials Becky's cell phone. "Hello, Becky."

"Yes, Bob," Becky says.

"Becky, get in your truck and go to my parents' house and pick up unit 601. I left it there."

"Where are you?"

"Becky, I will tell you later. Right now, go and pick up the unit and respond to station 2."

"Is Jerry over there?"

Bob suddenly realizes that Jerry could have gone over there. "Let's hope not."

"Okay, supe. I am en route." Becky jumps into her truck and raises a red flashing emergency light and places it on the roof of her truck. It sticks on with a magnetic ring at the bottom of it. She has used it countless of times when she had to respond on her days off. She flips a small light switch and hopes the emergency hideaway strobes work.

They turn on, and she whispers to herself, "Thanks, Jerry." Jerry had just worked on them and had gotten them to work. She arrives at Bob's parents' house and quickly jumps into Unit 601. She can hear all the traffic off the siren speakers. She starts the unit and turns on the emergency lights. She waits and then picks up the radio. She radios dispatch.

"Dispatch to all responding units, start to sound off your current location."

"Unit 636 is eastbound on Bitters Road, coming up on Mile 3 west."

"Kennedy County FD is eastbound on Bitters Road, coming up on Mile 4 west. Be advised I have our tanker truck on my six o'clock."

"Medic 2 is also eastbound, and I have the tanker about a half mile at my twelve o'clock."

"First responder, 601. Dispatch, can you log me down en route to station 2?"

"10-4, 601."

A convoy of light and sirens head down a county road. From a distance, it looks like a rope of light against the dark night background, twisting, following the winding road.

"Dispatch to all responding units, be advised downgrade to code 2 and use Thompson Pass to get there faster."

Bob looks at the radio and picks up the microphone. "101 to all responding units, delay that order and continue code 3."

"101 dispatch, do you have traffic?"

"101, negative, no traffic."

"Dispatch, you just advised us to downgrade to code 2 and take Thompson Pass."

"Negative. You are to continue code 3 to structure fire, and the route you use is at your discretion."

"10-4."

"Tommy, did you hear the traffic?"

"Yep, someone is on our frequency and trying to hurt us."

"601, 636."

"Go ahead, 601."

"I am taking Thompson Pass. Dispatch is right. It is closer. If Jerry is over there, he needs my help."

"601, do not use Thompson Pass."

"Sorry, supe. I have to do this."

"601. Okay, but be careful, try to slow down. There is a small cattle crossing that hasn't been used for a while."

"10-4."

Bob gets a feeling of Deja Vu. "Tommy, something is wrong."

"Bob, I know, but I will get to the bottom of it," Tommy says.

"That's not it. I have been here before." Bob grabs the microphone and radios Becky.

"101, 601."

"Go ahead."

"How close are you to Thompson Pass?"

"I am about a half a mile away."

"Becky, slow down," Bob says.

"Why?"

"Becky, listen to me, you need to start slowing down right now."

"Why, I am almost at station 2."

"Becky, slow down now!"

Becky hits the brakes once and then again and slows down. As she approaches the cattle crossing, she notices that the oil rig pipes used to construct the crossing are all routed out. She slams the brakes and stops just short of the drop-off. She gets off the truck and looks down at the crossing. She also finds that the rains have left a ten-foot gash in the road.

"601, 101," Becky says.

"Go ahead."

"You were right. The crossing is out, and there is a ten-foot drop in the road. That was close."

"10-4. 601 dispatch, I will be rerouting to station 2 through Bitters Road. For your 10-14 [for your information], the cattle crossing at Thompson Pass is 10-7 [out of service]. Could you have the county come by tomorrow and try to fix it?"

"10-4."

Tommy and Bob arrive at whatever is left of station 2. The building is partly on fire, and the natural-gas line is spewing flames about ten feet in the air. Firefighters quickly control the fire and shut off the gas to the building. Bob looks to his right and sees something moving in the grass.

It's Jerry, and he is badly burned. "Jerry!" Bob kneels down and holds him. The medics start to try to bandage the burns but know it is too late. Jerry is not going to make it. His legs are burnt to the bone. His face is half–burnt, and he has second- to third-degree burns to his abdomen.

Jerry is barely conscious. He feels no pain because the nerve endings are burned completely and dead. "Bob, I knew you would come."

"Jerry, just breathe. The ambulance will take you to the hospital in a minute."

The medics know that Bob is lying.

"Bob, can you believe it? I was going crazy. I know now that it is not real."

Bob replies, "You're right, Jerry it is not real."

Jerry smiles. "I knew it, but you have—" He starts to cough and coughs out blood from his mouth. "You have to watch out for one."

Jerry's body goes limp, and he stops breathing. The medics step in, but Bob stops them and shakes his head as if to say no, he is gone. Suddenly, Becky arrives on scene and runs toward Bob. She looks around him and sees Jerry's burned body and starts to scream. "No, Jerry, no! Bob, not Jerry."

Bob stops her from going and facing the burned body. "He's gone, Becky."

"No, Bob, we can bring him back, you can bring him back. You're the paramedic, you can bring him back."

"Becky, he is dead. Let him rest in peace."

Becky drops to her knees, and Bob stands over her. He whispers to her. "It's going to be all right." Bob takes a deep breath and asks the medics to help Becky stand up and take her to their ambulance. "Take her to the hospital, and have them see her there."

The radio comes on. "Medic 1 dispatch. Log us down en route to Kennedy County Heart Hospital, code one times one."

"10-4, Medic 1."

Bob jumps into Unit 601 and speeds away. "636, 101."

"101, do you need an escort to the County Heart Hospital?"

"636, hell, yes."

"Medic 1 dispatch, upgrading to code 3 times one." Bob is desperate now and finds that he can't drive fast enough to avoid what is currently happening to his father. He knows Frank is a good medic but still feels like he himself could do better. They both arrive at Kennedy County Heart Hospital and rush to the ambulance entrance. They are met by security and stop them before they can get to where they have Mr. Matt. They can see the doctor and nurses working on his father, and Bob turns away. He sees Frank sitting on the passenger side of Medic 1, and he runs over there. Tommy tries to stop him, but he pushes him aside. Frank looks up and sees Bob coming. He just sits there and doesn't move.

"Frank, what did you do?" Bob asks.

"Nothing, Bob," Frank says. "I'm sorry, but you're not going to blame us for this. I did everything I could for your dad."

Bob realizes that he is wrong and apologizes. "Frank, what happened? He was fine."

"I know. When we took off, your dad was talking and mentioning that you were the best kid anyone could have, and about halfway to the hospital, something happened."

"What are you talking about?"

"The lights in the back of the ambulance started to flicker. Black smoke started to come out of the AC vents."

"Was the ambulance on fire?" Bob asks.

"I yelled at Joe to check his dash, and he said everything was fine," Frank says. "Suddenly, your dad grabbed his chest and yelled out in pain. I looked over to my monitor, and he was in V-tach. I followed procedure, but I was having a hard time seeing because the lights started to flicker faster. I tried to apply the defibrillator pads, but they wouldn't stay on. That's when I noticed that the smoke was pulling them off."

"What are you saying?"

"I know it sounds weird, but that's what I saw. I went to advise Joe what I just saw, and I heard a strange noise. I turned around to see what was behind me, and it was Jerry. I could barely make him out due to the lights flickering. He looked at me and smiled. He said, 'Everything is going to be all right.' The smoke wrapped around him, and the back door to the ambulance opened, and Jerry jumped out. As Jerry jumped out, he whispered to me, 'It's not real.' I swear to God that is what happened."

Tommy begins to ask Frank where Joe was when the treating doctor walks outside and asks to speak with Bob. "Mr. Matt, your father is stable right now, but we are going to keep him for the rest of the weekend to monitor him. He is not out of the woods yet, but he is stable."

"Doctor, can I see him?" Bob asks.

"Sure, your mother is in there right now."

Tommy and Frank stay outside. Frank is advised of all the information about Jerry. Tommy asks Frank not to mention it to anyone until tomorrow. Bob spreads open the curtain and finds his dad in an unconscious state. His mom is close and gives him a kiss on the cheek. Bob takes a deep breath and joins his mother, and they both hug his father.

Bob slowly walks outside and sees Frank talking with Tommy. "Frank, get back in service. When you get back to the station, put Medic 1 out of service. Use Medic 2 for the rest of the shift. It's already 4:30 a.m. Try to get some sleep. And, Frank, you're a hell of a medic. I wouldn't have asked for a better job than the one you did on my father. Thanks."

Medic 1 is started, and they clear the scene.

"Are you okay to drive, Frank?" Joe asks.

"Yes, I'm okay," Frank says. "I'm tired, but I can drive. You know, Joe, with all that's going on, I can't help but remember about a call I had, about four years ago. I was working for a company called Rio Valley Emergency Medical Service. We were called out to a house for a possible gun-shoot victim. It was weird. The dispatcher advised us to respond code 1, as per the sheriff officers on the scene. We get there. Two officers are there, and a possible bystander. The bystander appeared to be in his thirties.

"The officers advised us that the victim was in the rose bushes. I remember the look on the man's face as I pasted him. He looked at me. There was no expression of pain, no regret. It looked like he was relieved. The poor victim was lying in a patch of roses. I remember seeing a thorn stuck in his cheek. I removed it, and I began to access the victim's vital signs.

"The mother arrived, and chaos began. She obviously was distraught at seeing her son lying in roses. It was hard to hear her crying for the loss of her son. I remember slipping on the stethoscope and completely blocking the chaos. I pumped up the blood pressure cuff, and I followed the needle up to 200. I then released the pressure, and there, in the faintest corner of the number 60, I hear a faint thump. I pulled off the stethoscope and advise my partner that the patient had a pulse. I don't remember if I yelled out to my partner, but no one turned around.

"My partner rushes to the ambulance and pulls the stretcher out. We load him on the unit. My partner is artificially breathing for him with a bag valve mask. The mother runs over and asks us to stop. 'No, ma'am, we can't stop.' The person who was standing and speaking with the officers runs over and also asks us to please stop. 'I know that it is your job to do whatever you have to help the patient, but there has to be a way you can stop. Our son has been suffering with depression all his life. This is not the first time he has been in a lifethreatening situation. We are tired, son. Please stop.'

"I remember calling the lead officer on the scene. I mentioned that I could only stop if he would accept responsibility for the patient, but if he accepts responsibility and he wanted us to stop, he would have to sign our refusal forms, which basically said that he elected to stop all life-saving measures. The officer accepts responsibility and then asks us to stop all efforts. The parents both thank us and the attending officers. I guess they figured that the patient was going to be a vegetable for the rest of his life.

"I remember going to the funeral and speaking with the father. He mentioned that they had lived with their son's depression all their life. There was danger at every corner with him. It seemed like his son knew what type of toll he was creating on his mother and him. He told me that afternoon was the longest time that he seemed normal in a long time.

"'He had asked us to the kitchen table, because he wanted to ask us a very important question. He asked us if he was the son we always wanted. "Oh yes, son."

I asked him if we were the parents he wished for. He smiled and said yes. After a while, he asked his mother if she could go get him some new shoes because he wanted to take a walk with us. She left, and I stayed to watch him. I was trimming the roses when he came and sat down beside me. We talked a little, and then he asked me if one day we could forgive him. I turned around and asked for what. That's when I saw him. He had the gun to his head. He asked me not to be scared, that this was his present to us. He said good-bye and pulled the trigger. I guess in his mind he saw himself as burden to us. I am sad because I wish I could have told him that I would have traded all the good days for one more bad day with him in our lives.'

"I never went back to visit with them again, but I guess I will do that tomorrow. I guess that stuck to me."

"Okay, partner, I will go with you," Joe says. "Let's do that tomorrow."

After about forty minutes on the road, Frank glances at the rearview mirror, and he sees something in the back of the ambulance box. He looks again, and a face appears on the opening to the rear box.

Franks yells out, "What the heck!" He pulls over and runs to the back of the ambulance and swings open the rear loading door and looks inside, trying to find a person.

Joe stands next to him, puzzled. "Partner, what did you see?"

"There was something in the back," Frank says.

Joe looks inside the box and sees nothing. "Partner, you're tired. Maybe that's what it is."

"Joe, don't start with me. I know what I saw."

"I believe you, but why don't I drive the rest of the way? When we get back to the station, we both will look for whatever you saw." Joe gets into the driver's seat, and they leave the area.

THEY ALL WILL PAY

They finally arrive back at the station. Joe parks the unit outside. "Frank, don't worry about the ambulance equipment. Just go to bed, and I will take care of it."

"Are you sure?" Frank asks.

"Just go to bed, you weenie. Let the real men do the work."

"Does the real man want to do the report for Mr. Matt?" Frank asks.

"I don't think so," Joe says.

"That's where the real men become mice."

They both start to laugh.

"Good night."

Joe begins to move the large equipment first. He moves the backboards and moves the heart monitor. He moves the trauma bags and O2 bags. He stops to catch his breath and wonders where in the hell did they get so much equipment, and do they use it at all? He stops and lights up a cigarette and inhales a large puff of smoke. He leans on Medic 3's hood and looks at the new ambulance.

He suddenly hears children's voices. It sounds like they are laughing. Underneath the chassis, he can see little feet run back and forth from the front to the back. He finds it strange that little kids would be out so early in the morning. He shouts to them, "Okay, you kids, now you are in trouble. I called the police, and they are on their way. You guys better not be here when they arrive. The police will take you to jail."

The little feet stop. One set of feet start to go toward the back of the ambulance. Just before the feet come around the corner, they stop.

Joe sees something coming from behind the station. It's Jerry. "Hey, Joe, what's up?"

"Jerry, what are you doing this early in the morning?"

"I was driving around, thinking."

"I didn't see your car in the parking lot."

I parked it a little ways up the street."

"So, what's up, dude?" Joe asks.

"Need some help moving equipment?" Jerry asks.

"Sure, thanks."

They begin to move all the equipment out of Medic 1 and into Medic 3. "Well, we are done. Thanks, Jerry, for everything. You want to come in?"

"No I have to go, but I will see you around, okay?" Jerry says.

"See you later." Joe enters the ambulance bay area and closes the garage door. He turns the lights off and retires to bed. Outside the building, Jerry stands by the Medic 1. You can see he is talking to someone. Underneath the chassis, you can see two feet stand there. Jerry turns toward the station and smiles. He then turns to the person, and a little girl is standing there.

Jerry tells her, "It is not their fault. You need to leave."

She replies, "Yes, it is their fault. They were paramedics." Her voices changes. "So they all pay for killing my brothers and sister."

"No," Jerry says. "As long as I am here, you are not hurting anyone anymore!"

The little innocent girl transforms into a hellish figure. Claws stretch out from her fingers, and her face turns black. Fangs protrude out of her mouth. Suddenly, she hears a voice. A little boy stands behind her and asks, "Lucy, I am hungry. Is there anything to eat?"

She changes back to the innocent little girl and picks him up. "Now, Billy, come with me, and I'll make you something to eat." She turns back to Jerry and says, "I will make all of them pay."

The children disappear into the night. Jerry stands there and watches them disappear. He whispers to himself, "Not on my watch."

Frank is in the back of the ambulance. The lights are flickering faster and faster. He can only see his movements in sections. Like he was in slow motion, he stares at his hands, and they turn black and then turn to smoke. He looks up toward the stretcher, and Jerry is there. Jerry is all burned.

Suddenly, Jerry opens his eyes and grabs Frank. He yells out, "Frank, Frank!"

Frank opens his eyes, and Joe is waking him up. "Frank, wake up. Hey, partner, good morning. We have to go. The morning crew is here, and we have to get ready."

"Good morning," Frank says.

"Did you have a bad dream?" Joe asks.

"Sort of."

"Well, you were tossing and turning."

"Sorry. Did you get to finish changing the stuff off the ambulances?"

"Yes. You won't believe how much stuff we have in the units. Luckily, Jerry showed up and gave me a hand."

"What?" Frank exclaims.

Joe turns to look at Frank and answers again. "Jerry gave me a hand, and we finished moving all the stuff."

Frank sits down and holds his head. "This can't be happening."

"What's wrong, Frank?"

"Joe, don't you know what happened last night? Weren't you paying attention?"

"Yes. Station 2 burned down."

"That's all you heard? Where were you?"

"Well, if you must know, I was with the nurse from ER. We were making out in her car, and I must have left the radio in the ambulance."

"Joe, Jerry is gone," Frank says. "He is dead. He was at station 2 when it blew up. He burned to death."

"Then who was helping me?" Joe asks.

"Are you sure it was Jerry?"

"Yes. I saw him as close as you sitting there. It was Jerry."

The door opens, and the incoming crew member walks in. "Did I interrupt something?"

Bob is awake to see the sun rise. He has been with his parents at the hospital all night, and it is now morning. He sips on a cup of the most awful coffee he's ever tasted. He thinks about what has happened in the past twenty-four hours. *Is it finally here?* he asks himself. *Will it finally show its face?*

He dares it. He finally feels that he is ready to face it. "Whatever you are, I am ready. You are not hurting anyone anymore.

Bob's cell phone begins to ring. It is George White. Bob takes a moment. He takes a deep breath and answers. "Hello, George?"

"Hello, Bob? What is happening?"

"I trust that you found out about station 2."

"What happened to Jerry?"

"Jerry is dead, George. He died in the explosion. I guess he went there to talk to me. When he turned the lights on, the building exploded. Apparently, there was a natural-gas leak inside the building."

"Oh my god!"

"George, I need to call everyone in to work," Bob says. "I also need the office staff as well. I know that this is going to be expensive, but I need this to happen."

"Sure, I understand."

"I will be en route to station 1 in about an hour. I have to say bye to my parents."

"How is your father doing?" George asks.

"He's okay right now, but he is not out of the woods yet. Right now, I need everyone to come in."

"Okay, Bob, I'll get right on it."

Bob walks back in and enters the examination room.

His dad is asleep, and his mother is by his father's side. She tells Bob not to worry. She will call him if anything changes. "Go and help your friends, son. They need you more right now. I know that you love your father, and he knows it too."

"I love you, Mom," Bob says.

His mother replies, "I love you more."

Bob kisses her good-bye and walks out and to unit 601.

THE NEW BOSS

Bob arrives at station one. The parking area is filled with cars and trucks. He has to park the unit next to the building on a grassy area. He walks in to the building, and everyone goes silent when they see him come in. He walks over to Sandra and asks her where George is. As Bob walks to George's office, he passes Becky. He looks at her, and she gives him a thumb up.

Bob walks into George's office. George is sitting next to his desk. He has his head down and is having trouble with the whole situation. "Bob, I can't do this. I thought I could handle it, but I can't."

"Hold on, George," Bob says. "Everyone is here, and I will take over from here."

"Bob, that's not what I mean. I have no EMS experience. Half the time, I don't know what is going on to try to help, and if it wasn't for you, I would have killed someone!"

"Okay, George, maybe you need a break from this. Take a vacation or something."

"Oh, Bob. You don't get it, do you?" George hands Bob a letter.

"You can't do this," Bob says.

"Yes, I can, and I am doing it. Bob, you were meant for this. This is what you live for. Everyone respects you and will follow you anywhere. This is my last day as the owner of Orion Emergency Medical Service, but this is your first as the head of this great company."

"Why are you doing this, George? I don't know how to run this business."

"In the last twenty-four hours, you have done more for this company and its employees than I have in ten years of owning it, but I am slowly changing that. If you read the second page, you will find that I started breaking ground on a new station. Remember the meeting I was having with the bank? They finally approve the financing and construction of the new EMS station. Bob, I was hoping that you will allow me to continue on as the manager of the office personnel. I won't take no for an answer. If you say no, I will give it to Greg. I know we both don't want that."

They both laugh, and George leaves the office. Bob sits down and tries to control his emotions. He looks down at the desk and notices a flier under some papers. He pulls the flier and reads it. It reads, "Southwest Community College." He opens the flier and finds a new student application to attend the college's

EMT program. He smiles and reads the name on the application: George White.

Bob calls Sandra on the intercom to see him in Mr. White's office.

"Yes, Robert, you asked for me?" Sandra says.

"Yes, Sandra. Come in and sit down, please."

"What's up? Did I do something wrong?"

Bob smiles and replies, "Sandra, due to recent events, I have to advise you that I—or rather, *we* cannot see each other after hours in any way shape or form. I am really sorry that I have to tell you this. The thought of getting to know you personally was very important to me. I know that I must sound like an idiot to you and you might not want to talk to me anymore, but I hope you will understand."

"Robert, I do understand, but can I ask you a personal question?" Sandra says. "If anything happens between me and you in the years to come, will you fight it and stay away?"

Bob smiles and replies, "There is no way I will fight it. I can almost guarantee it."

Becky is called over the intercom.

"What do you need, Bob?"

"Becky, there are changes being made, and one of them is you. I am making you a supervisor, and I hope that you are ready for it. I trust that you will act responsible and take care of your crews. That is all I have for you. Could you ask Greg to come to my office, please?"

"Thanks, Bob," Becky says. "I won't let you down." As she leaves, you can see that she has a smile on her face.

Greg enters the room and sits down. Bob is standing and has his back toward him. "Greg I have known you for about three years now, and you have never failed to surprise me. I believe in how you handle yourself, your crews, and up until two days ago, I wasn't going to do what I am about to do now."

You can see Greg start to get nervous and sweat. Bob turns around, and Greg interrupts, "Please don't fire me, sir. I know that I can be a dumb guy, but I can do better."

Bob starts to laugh. "Greg, I am not firing you. You are my new lead supervisor. I always thought that you were a weird, and I figured you wouldn't last, but you surprised me. You will basically take over my position, and I hope that you are up for the challenge. Please keep it to yourself until I make the announcement. Congratulations, Greg."

Bob shakes Greg's hand. "Greg, could you have everybody assemble in the bay area? I have a couple of announcements to make."

"Okay, everybody, quiet down," Bob says. "First, I want to advise everyone that last night, this ambulance service lost a good paramedic, and I lost a dear friend. I had the honor of working with him at several other companies, and each time we moved, we grew closer and closer. Jerry to me was like a little brother. I will miss him a lot, and I know some of you will too."

He turns toward Becky. "We should continue what he started and hope that he is in a much better place. Reverend Michael is here to say a prayer for Jerry and his family. After the prayer, we will step outside and sound our siren for Jerry and call out for his badge for the last time."

They all bow their heads and say a prayer. The siren on both Medic 2 and 3 are sounded. Becky hugs Bob and starts to cry. Everyone turns to each other and hug one another. Bob looks around and sees Tommy standing in the parking lot. They all walk back in, and Bob advises everyone where the funeral services will be held and when the procession is going to be. He asks everyone to take a ten-minute break and rejoin back in the bay area.

•••◦▸━━━━━●━━━━━◂◦•••

"Okay, everyone, I have several announcements to make," Bob says. "The first is Greg Stafford will be assuming my position as lead supervisor. I expect everyone to show him the same respect you've shown me. Let's have a big round of applause for Greg."

Everyone claps and yells out, "Congratulations, Greg!"

"Next," Bob says. "Now that Greg has moved up, we will be missing a new supervisor. I had to make a rush decision, and I am proud to announce our new supervisor to take Greg's position, Becky Rodriguez. I trust that she will gain your respect and help push this company forward. Let's give her a round of applause."

Everyone claps their hands and yells out, "Good job, supe."

"Okay, I know that all of you are wondering what about me," Bob says. "Well, I have been entrusted with the keys to Orion EMS, and I humbly accepted. Mr. White has stepped down as the owner and elected to take over as manager of the office personnel. Before stepping down, Mr. White has made me aware that with wisdom and persuasive powers, he has gotten the bank to start breaking new ground on our new station. I want to say that as the new owner of Orion EMS, together we can accomplish everything."

Sandra walks over and gives Bob a hug and congratulates him.

Bob sees Becky walking outside and follows her outside. "Becky."

"Yes, sir."

"I have an assignment for you."

"What is it, sir?"

"Can you meet me at my parents' house this afternoon?"

"Sure, Mr. Matt."

Tommy approaches Bob. "Hey, Bob. How does it feel holding the reins?"

"How did you know?" Bob asks.

"Remember when you politely asked me to take George home because he was drunk?" Tommy says. "He told me all about it and asked me for my opinion. I told him not to. I guess he didn't follow my suggestion, but he told me to keep it to myself."

"You knew all this time, and you didn't tell me," Bob says. "Hey, Tommy, are you off today?"

"No, but I can be."

"Can you meet me at my parents' house this afternoon?"

"Sure, see you there."

Bob feels he is now ready to tackle these strange things that have been going on.

THE INVESTIGATION

Bob sits on his dad's old rocking chair. He is waiting for his partners to arrive. As he rocks back and forth, he realizes that the chair is so comfortable. The armrests are faded, and the color is like old leather. The pressed wood is coming apart because the clear varnish has all but vanished. Small areas still look shiny, but they are few and far between. The chair is still sturdy, which reminds Bob of his father.

Tommy arrives first and has with him a small ice chest. By the way he is carrying it, it might be full. "Hey, Bob, do you want a drink?"

"No."

"Relax, it's a soft drink."

"Well, in that case, give me an Orange soda."

Becky arrives carrying three pizza boxes. "Tommy called me to bring some food."

"There is a reason I asked you guys here," Bob says. "I wanted to know if you would like to help me with this thing that has been bugging me. As you guys know, there have been a lot of weird things happening here, and I have to find out what it is. I know you two are aware of what I am talking about, but before we can begin to investigate, I need to confirm one last thing. Right now, Larry, our mechanic, is checking Medic 1, and I am waiting for his call. If I am correct, we will know where to begin.

"Tommy, you know, being an police officer, if there is anybody involved, you can arrest the individual. Becky, you were the last person with Jerry before he went in to shock. Myself, I have my father and Frank's story."

Bob's cell phone begins to ring. It is Larry. He puts the phone on speaker. "Hello, Larry?"

"Bob?"

"Larry. What did you find on the ambulance?"

"Bob, as far as the unit itself, there is nothing wrong with it," Larry says. "I checked it completely, and I found nothing wrong. I went ahead and went through it again, and I found several things. I don't know if these are the things you are looking for, but did you know that this ambulance has no actual radio in the front cab?"

"Larry, the unit has the buttons and the microphone in the front cab."

"Yes, but it is a remote unit," Larry says. "The actual radio is in the box. The antenna and power, everything is in the box. The other thing is inside the inner wall of the aluminum module box. It looks like it had been painted black, or so I thought. When I went to scrub it, I noticed that it was cooked on, and the black color wasn't paint at all. It looks like burnt insulation and something else. I don't know what it is, but it looks funny.

"The last thing I found was hard to detect. I had missed it on the last two times I checked this unit. When you told me to leave no stone unturned, I found it. I found a small area that had paint overspray. At first, it wasn't a big deal, but I started thinking. When a manufacturer builds these units, they paint the module box and the vehicle chassis apart from each other. After they are painted, all the gaskets are added and applied over the paint. The area I found was between the rear window of the cab and the access hole of the module box. The bellow had a little tiny spot of overspray at the bottom. The ambulance has been remounted."

"What does that mean?" Bob asks.

"What it means is the truck chassis is newer than the module box," Larry answers. "Right now, I have my guys trying to find an actual stamped date anywhere on the box."

"Larry, it's Tommy Reiner," Tommy says. "Did you pull some of the material from inside of the box? The black stuff you found, did you save some?"

"Way ahead of you," Larry says. "It is in a plastic bag."

"I will be over to your place as soon as I can," Tommy says.

"Okay, Tom," Larry says. "Bob, I am completely taking this unit apart. Are you sure you want me to do this, and how long do you want me to be here?"

"Do whatever you need to, and I don't care how much it cost in over time. Just find everything you can!"

"Okay, boss. I will call you if I find a date or anything else."

"Okay, Larry. Bye." Bob turns to both Tommy and Becky. "Okay, now I have something for us to check. My dad has been working on his car for about four years now, and I want you two to look at what he has done so far. I saw something, and I want you guys to take a look at the car. I want to know if you see what I see."

They walk over to the garage, and they all stand at distance. Tommy goes first. "Well, I see a muscle car with no fenders. The fenders are off because it's being restored. The seats are out of the car because again it is being restored. The engine compartment and engine have parts taken off, because it is being restored."

"Wait a minute, why would your father being doing that?" Becky asks.

Tommy replies, "Because he was restoring the car."

"No, that's not what I mean," Becky says. "My brother was restoring an old car two years ago. He would spend hours on it. He had parts over there and other parts over here, but what I remember is that he would have old parts in one area and the new parts in another. If the front fenders were off, he would have the new ones in the general area. What I see here is that Mr. Matt was possibly taking the car apart. I don't see any new parts. All I see is parts taken off."

Bob smiles and replies, "Exactly right, Becky. Last year, I gave my father two thousand dollars to help with restoration, and I don't see any new parts. The parts he has taken off are rusty but not enough to replace them. Look at the fenders. They look original, with no rust at all. He has them in a pile ready to be thrown away. Then I ask myself why would he be dismantling the car? That's the question I have for my mother.

"Becky, what I want you to do is check in the public library, or wherever you can, for old newspapers. Look for anything which deals with an ambulance or with EMS personnel. I have a feeling that what we are dealing with is a thing from the past. Something happened here, and it's come back to haunt us. It's already taken Jerry, and I will not let it take my dad!"

Tommy leaves to pick up the evidence Larry has for him, and Becky leaves to try to find old newspapers. Bob sits back on the rocking chair and watches both of them leave.

Tommy arrives at Larry's shop and enters the building. All the lights are on, but he can't see anyone. He calls out for Larry, and no one answers. He walks over to where Medic 1 is and sees no one is there working on it. He unsnaps his side arm and slowly walks to the office area inside the building. He grabs his cell phone and calls Bob. "Hello, Bob?"

"Tommy?"

"Bob, I am here at Larry's shop, and I can't find anyone. All the tools are out. Lights are all on, but there is no one here. I am going to check out the office."

"Tommy, be careful," Bob says. "We don't know what we are dealing with. Call for backup."

Tommy does just that. "636. Dispatch."

"636. Go ahead."

"I am currently at Fifth Street and Washington at Larry's shop. I need a code 1017 at my location. Advise the responding officer that I am in plain clothes."

Tommy slowly walks over to the office area. He can hear a person whispering something from inside the office.

"Hello?" Tommy calls out. "This is a sheriff officer. Are you hurt? Are you in there, Larry?" Tommy draws his weapon. He ducks down and slowly opens the door. He aims his weapon to the front of him and turns on a small flashlight. The office is pitch-black. To the far end of the office, he can barely make out a person. He shines the light at the area, and he sees a small girl slumped over somebody. Just then he notices that it is Larry.

The little girl turns her head around, and Tommy is horrified. Her face is dark in color. Fangs protrude out of her mouth. Tommy notices that she has turned only her head completely, and her torso is still facing Larry. Tommy jumps back and struggles to regain his footing. The thing now claws her way over Larry's steel desk. As she claws her way over the steel surface of the desk, you can hear catlike scratching noises as she reaches toward Tommy. Larry tries to stand up, and the thing turns its head toward Larry.

Tommy yells at Larry, "Don't move!"

Suddenly, you hear several voices and patrol cars arriving with a screeching stop. The thing disappears in a puff of smoke. Larry stands up and runs out the office. Tommy yells out to the officers, "Don't shoot!" But it is too late. In a loud bang, Larry is hit and falls to the floor.

Tommy yells out, "Sheriff Officer, don't shoot!" He runs over to Larry.

Larry is still alive. The shot nicked his throat. Tommy calls on the radio for an ambulance. "636 dispatch, we have a man down. We need an ambulance ASAP!"

"10-4. EMS is en route."

In the background, you can hear the ambulance calling en route. "Orion Medic 3 en route code 3."

Another emergency vehicle arrives; it is Bob in unit 601. "Tommy, are you okay?"

Tommy is sitting in a shop chair.

"Tommy, what happened?" Bob asks.

"I don't know," Tommy says. "I will tell you when I figure it out."

"What are you talking about?"

"Look, Bob, I have to figure it out first, and then I will let you know. What I can tell you is that we are fighting something very strange, and I am not sure how we are going to do it. When I figure it out, I will tell you."

An officer brings a plastic bag and gives it to Tommy. "Was this the evidence you were looking for?"

Tommy takes the bag. "Right now, I have to get this evidence to the lab. When I get the results, I will call you."

"Okay, Tom," the officer says. "I am going to the hospital and see if I can get something from Larry."

Tommy leaves the scene, and Bob takes off the hospital.

As Bob drives to the hospital, he gets a call from Becky.

"Hello, Bob?"

"Hey, Becky, did you find something?"

"Yes. Where are you?"

"I am en route to the hospital," Bob says. "Larry accidentally got shot. I have to go see him and try to find out what happened at his shop. What did you find?"

"I am going over there, and I will let you know when I see you."

"Okay, be careful."

Tommy arrives at the county lab and hands the evidence over. "Hey, guys, I need to know how fast you can work on getting this evidence figured out for me."

"It should take about an hour," the lab tech mentions.

"Then I'll wait. Do you have a snack machine?" Tommy asks.

Becky arrives at the hospital to meet with Bob.

"Becky," Bob asks, "What did you find?"

Becky asks, "What did you get from Larry?"

"Larry's throat was injured, and we can't get anything from him till he heals."

Becky explains, "Well I went to the library, but it was closed. I know the security guy there. He's always had a thing for me since high school. Anyway, I couldn't find anything at first. I checked for ambulances and for businesses which were EMS related, and you won't believe what I found. In 1970, there used to be an ambulance service called Code 2 Emergency Medical Service. The owners were both medics, and they serviced both Kennedy County and ours. They only had one ambulance, and for the most part, they did an okay job.

"Well, as luck would have it, Arcadian EMS come in and completely took over the area, and they were forced to close. I thought that it was done, but then I read another paper dated almost a year later. It told readers of a tragic accident involving an ambulance and a car. The accident left four kids dead. They were burned alive in an ambulance that was converted into a motor home. I didn't notice the connection until I saw the pictures of the vehicles. Bob, look at the car the ambulance hit."

Bob stares in surprise. The picture shows a car exactly like the car his dad was working on. The story read that the car was owned by a person with a last name of Matt. Bob grabs his cell phone and calls his mother. "Hello, Mom?"

"Yes, Bobby."

"Where did Dad buy the car he has in the garage from?"

"I don't know, son. He had that car since before we were married. Every time I would ask him, he would get frustrated and storm out of the house. After a while, I stopped asking him anything about the car. Why do you ask?"

"No reason. I was just wondering. How is he doing?"

"He is much better," Bob's mother says. "He opened his eyes and talked to me for a little bit."

"Mom, make sure that you call me if anything changes." Bob hangs up the phone.

"What did she say?" Becky asks.

"She doesn't know anything," Bob answers. "We need to get more information on that car." He calls Tommy on the phone. "Hello, Tommy?"

"Bob, go ahead."

"Tommy, where can we get information on an old auto accident which involved deaths?"

"Where did it happen?" Tommy asks.

"The accident happened on Farm Road 220 and Old Baggers Road. According to a newspaper report, it happened in 1970."

"That is in our county. I will go to the main station and start to look there. If you can get the vehicle identification number of the car, call me with it."

Becky continues with her search. "The parents of the kids were tried and sentenced to life in prison with no parole. Bob, they are still alive and in prison. We have to go and talk to them about what is happening here."

"Tommy would have to go with us because they won't allow us to see them," Bob says. "Let's wait till Tommy calls, and we will ask him then."

Bob's mother calls him on the phone. "Bobby, your father is awake and is calling for you."

"I will be right there." Bob asks Becky to wait and hands her his cell phone. "Take my phone. If Tommy calls, answer. I do not want you to leave without me, Becky."

"Okay, Bob. Please be gentle with your father."

Bob walks into the room where his father is being treated, and asks his mother to please give them a few minutes. His dad tells him that whatever it is, his mother needs to hear it too.

"Dad, whatever I ask you, today I want you to be honest," Bob says. "And no matter how hard it may be on our emotions, you have to answer all the questions."

"Son, I have been waiting for this day for a long time," Bob's father says. "When you asked me about the car lot, I knew that it would be a matter of time when you would figure things out. So before you ask me any questions, let me tell you and your mother my story. You can ask any question you want after that.

"In 1970, I was a senior in high school. Your grandfather had made me work all that summer and then gave me all the money I earned to buy a new car. A car dealer had opened a new lot just outside of town. The car lot was on FM 220 and Old Baggers Road.

He had very nice-looking cars, but I set my eyes on a 1968 Dodge Coronet R/T convertible. I went in, and within an hour, I was in the car of my dreams. I went and picked up some of my friends to cruise the town.

"At about 4:00 p.m., I drop them off and went to Cindy Johnson's house and showed her the car. Her family was there, and they all were surprised that I had bought the car. We took a ride around town for a while with her family. We returned, and we went inside the house. It was about 6:30 p.m. Cindy and I were on her porch talking about where we would go the following day. She asked if she could drive. I playfully said no way. If I would have known what was going to happen, I would have never allowed her to take the car.

"She grabbed the keys and ran to the car. I stayed on the porch, believing she wouldn't take the car. She asked if I would dare her to drive. I finally said, 'I dare you,' and she took off. As she took off, she yelled that she would return in an hour. She never returned. She was involved in an accident with a couple driving an ambulance which had been converted into a motor home. She was thrown out of the car and landed headfirst on the pavement. She died instantly.

"The children that were in the makeshift motor home weren't so lucky. They died a horrible death. They burned alive in the back of the motor home. The module box caught fire. The fire turned off by itself. The local fire department reported that the fire turned off because it finished all the oxygen and suffocated itself, but not before completely burning the children into dust. Some of the eyewitnesses reported that you could see the children banging on the doors and windows, yelling and screaming, 'Please let us out!' The insurance fixed the car, but after that, I couldn't drive the car anymore. The thought of those children being burned alive in the ambulance, and Cindy's death, made me decide to dismantle the car.

"I know that I have misled both of you, and for that, I sincerely apologize. I hope, honey, that you can forgive me for not being completely honest with you. I have held this inside of me, and it has been tearing a hole in my heart. I am glad that you figured it out, son, because I don't know how much longer I could have lived with it inside."

"When I married you, I married all of you, good or bad," Bob's mother says. "I would have hoped that you would have told me what was hurting you, and maybe I could have helped you. I guess God works in mysterious ways and makes us see that he does exist. I forgave you the moment I said I do, but in the future, remember I am your friend and your partner. Nothing can get in the middle of that unless we allow it."

Bob's parents both hug and gently kiss each other.

"Now, son, do you have any questions?" Bob's father asks.

Bob smiles. "No, you answered them all. I have to go and meet with Tommy. Mom, don't forget to call me if anything changes."

Bob leaves the room and goes to meet with Becky, who is waiting for him.

"Hey, Bob, Tommy called about five minutes ago and asked us to meet him at the county lab," Becky says. "He says that they got something from the evidence off Medic 1."

"Becky, I already know what they are going to tell us." Bob dials Tommy's cell phone. "Hello, Tommy?"

"Yes?" Tommy says.

"Tommy, could you meet us at Diana's Restaurant? Bring the results with you."

"10-4."

Bob and Becky leave and go to meet with Tommy at the restaurant.

They arrive at Diana's Restaurant and get a table. Tommy arrives shortly after, and they gather at the small table.

"Okay, guys," Tommy says. "The lab discovered that Larry was right. The hard black stuff is insulation that is burned. The heat got so intense that the insulation turned into glass, trapping the black stuff that you can see. When they managed to separate the glass from the black stuff, they were surprised to find that the chemical was human DNA. The human DNA fused with the insulation as it turned into glass, thus trapping the DNA like in a cocoon. The glass then tried to adhere to the inner aluminum wall of the ambulance."

Bob interrupts, "I knew it."

"Bob, how would you know?"

"Guys, my dad put everything together." Bob begins to tell them the story his father had told him.

After the story, Becky asks, "So now what are we going to do?"

"We are going to try to see if we can get the parents of the children out of jail," Bob says.

Tommy stands up and interrupts the meeting. "I am going to pretend I didn't hear that."

Bob grabs his arm and asks him to sit down "If you have a better solution, then let us know."

Tommy sits down and starts to think. "Becky, you and Bob mentioned that the parents were taken to trial and convicted for involuntary manslaughter, for acting on converting the ambulance into a motor home, which caused the death of their children, right?"

"Yes," Becky says.

"Then we have to look into the trial papers if anyone checked the ambulance itself," Tommy says. "If I am correct, neither the court nor the prosecutor checked the ambulance to see that if, in fact, the ambulance had a short circuit. This means that we can get the parents out of jail to hear new evidence. Worst-case scenario, the court doesn't allow the new evidence, but it does allow the parents to be brought to our jail and wait for a trial date. We can help them post bail, and they can help us with their children."

Bob smiles. "That is real good, Tommy."

"Now I don't know if this is proper procedure, but it is a lot better than trying to break someone out of prison," Tommy says. "What I want you to do, Bob, is go back to the hospital. Call me from there. You want to report new evidence regarding an old case. I will send one of my men to take down the information. He will, in turn, bring the report to me. I will then go to the district attorney and let him know of the report, and he will have to inform the courts. They will have to set a trial date. But they will also have to bring the parents to our jail. A bond will be set, and there you have it."

Becky replies, "How long will this take?"

"Well, I'm guessing about a week or so," Tommy says.

"That's too long," Becky says. "We have to push it along, Tommy. What do you think, Bob?"

"Becky, Tommy is right," Bob says. "If it takes a week or two, it won't make a difference as long as we get the parents here, and if anybody asks, you tell them that it came from Larry. Larry's voice got better for a bit, and he told us about the shorted wires. Besides, the district attorney is Tommy's cousin."

They all smile.

MEET THE CHILDREN
AND THE PARENTS

Within three days, the children parents are transported to the county jail, and a bond is set. Becky and Bob go to see them at the county jail.

"Hello, Mr. and Mrs. Richards. You don't know us, but we are here to help you."

"Is it true? They found new evidence."

"We did find something. The ambulance you used to have, I am afraid that we ended up with it."

"How did that happen? It was really old, and it was in an accident."

"First, we want to say that we know what happened to you and your children, and we feel real sorry for your loss, but I am afraid that we have met your children and we need your help."

"What are you talking about? Our children are dead. They died a long time ago, and it was our fault. What sick joke are you trying to pull?"

"Trust us, Mr. Richards, this is no joke, and we have reason to believe that what happened to your children wasn't your fault. If you would hear us out, you will understand why we are here."

Bob begins to tell them what they have seen and what they have found. After the story, Becky asks Mrs. Richards, "Can you tell us about your children? We think it is important that we get to know your children, especially Lucy."

———————

"Lucy was our first. She was very tiny, but a real fighter. She was born one month premature. The doctors didn't think she would survive. She almost didn't, but she fought, and slowly her lungs grew stronger. It took her almost three months before the hospital allowed us to take her home. She learned to walk real young. She would always follow us around. She didn't stop there. She learned to talk, and that was it. She was always trying to be in charge, and we encouraged it.

"Peter arrived, and Lucy would help take care of him. We knew that she was too young, but she would be very good at taking care of him. Josie arrived a year later. She was a little flower. She dressed up, asked for dresses and shoes with high heels. She would dance for us, entertain the whole family, and would convince Peter to act with her in plays she would do for us. William arrived when we had just started the ambulance company. It was really rough for us. We hardly had time for the kids anymore. Lucy stepped in and took charge. For a little while, we were doing fine. We had bought a new house, and we were already planning on buying a second ambulance. Then came Arcadian Emergency Medical Service. They came in and started taking over everything. It looked like we were going to survive because we covered a small area. It was too small to even look at, but they came after it.

"After several attempts, they convinced some board members, and they had what they wanted. We were left out. We both had put everything we had into it, and in one night, everything we dreamed about was gone. We both took it really hard. We told ourselves that we had enough money to last until we could find a job. Since we had put up a hard fight against Arcadian EMS, they would not hire us at all. The money slowly was spent on the new house and the bills until it was all gone. We lost the house, and we were evicted. We decided to convert the only ambulance we had into a motor home. The kids loved it. We would sleep in it and at different places. Whatever little money made was washing cars here and there.

"It started to get harder and harder for us. We had to go to court several times because we would leave the children unattended. We had no other choice. We finally couldn't handle it, and we started drinking.

The kids would have very little to eat. Lucy would find something for them and feed them. I was too drunk to do anything. The day of the accident was the only day we had not drunk. It was Josie's birthday, and Lucy had asked us not to drink.

"We were headed to the city park. Josie had a surprise play, and everyone had a part in it. Josie handed us a paper with our lines through the attendant window, and Brian reached to get it when we saw a car swerve in our direction. I saw the young girl's face as the car approached. She was trying to hold on and had the car's wheels locked in a skid. In a split second, it was over. Her car was embedded in the front of the ambulance. We were okay. I called to the children, and Lucy cried out, 'We are okay, Mom.' I opened the door and stepped out of the ambulance. I saw the young girl lying there on the street and I could not find any emotion to match what I was seeing. She too had no emotion. She had a streak of blood running down her right cheek; her eyes were open and glassy. Her blonde hair looked matted, with an area of red roots. For a second I hoped that she wouldn't move. I kept looking and waiting for arms to flex to begin to lift her body and assess her severe injuries. I wondered, if she only saw the large laceration on the top of her head, she wouldn't move, but according to the good Samaritans, she wasn't breathing. I quickly changed my attention to the children. I tried to open the side door to the module box, and it was locked. Brian tried to open the back loading doors, and they were locked too.

"We started smelling smoke and then seeing smoke coming from the module box. We tried to get the children through the access window, but fire was blocking the hole. Cars stopped and people tried to help, but we couldn't open the doors. We could see our babies hitting the small windows on the doors and screaming, yelling for help. Slowly their voices grew silent. Every inch of us wanted to tear through those doors, but we couldn't. The fire department arrived and used the Jaws of Life to open the doors. The fire had drowned itself. Not before consuming our babies.

"Nothing was left of them. We were tried and convicted within a couple of weeks. We didn't fight them at all. We were at fault, and we knew it. There was nothing to live for anymore. We had hoped for the death penalty, but the people said no. Too many deaths had happened, and two more was not going to heal any wounds."

Becky wipes the tears from her eyes. "Mr. and Mrs. Richards, you were not at fault, and we will help you make everyone see it. Your children were lucky that God left both of you to introduce them to the public. Mrs. Richards, I am very proud to have met your children."

Becky hugs Mrs. Richards, and Bob shakes Mr. Richards's hand.

The following day, Becky walks over to Tommy's office and delivers a banknote. "Officer Reiner, I am here to place bond for the Richards family."

Tommy smiles. "Ms. Rodriguez, please have a seat, and I will begin the process."

Within an hour, Mr. and Mrs. Richards walk out of the county jail. They step out very reluctantly but finally step into the sun. Mr. Richards takes a deep breath and turns to Becky and now Bob. "Don't know what we have done to deserve your help, but we both thank you very much. We both are ready to help in any way we can."

"We managed to rent an apartment for you, but the ambulance personnel want to meet you. If you don't mind, can we take you there? They want to convey their sympathy for the loss of your children."

They get in Bob's truck, and they drive toward station 1.

As they drive to the station, they pass the local church. Mrs. Richards asks if they can stop. Bob slows down and pulls into the church parking lot. The church is beautiful. The stained-glass windows add the final touch to a classic church appearance. They all walk in and approach the altar. The church interior is beautiful as well. You can see above the altar a painted picture of Jesus on a cross. On either side of the church walls are the stained-glass windows. The stained-glass windows have pictures of saints.

The sunlight passes through, sending different colors on to the pews. The pews are constructed of thick heavy solid wood. A faint wind moves dust particles into a swirl, and the particles gently begin to fall on the pews, but before they can land, they are violently moved again into a swirl by the same faint wind. The particles are only visible as the sun's rays refract through the stained glass and into the open hall inside the church. The stain on the pews appears to be old and gives the pews an antique look.

The hall is empty and quiet. Reverend Michael is busy wiping down the windows at the far end of the hall. "Welcome to the house of the Lord."

Becky walks over and tells Reverend Michael the story of the children and the Richards family. Mrs. Richards walks over to him and asks, "Can we pray, Father?"

"Yes, my daughter."

"Pray for us, Father, and for our children, for they are not been put to rest."

Reverend Michael asks them to bow their heads and begins the prayer. After they pray, he tells them, "As a reverend of this community, I want to offer my help with anything you may need." He adds, "May God guide you and keep you safe. Amen."

After meeting with the EMS personnel, Bob and Becky leave the Richards at the apartment complex.

"Well, good night. We will see you tomorrow. Officer Tommy Reiner will meet with us, and we will go to the mechanic's shop. The ambulance is there."

"I am looking forward to seeing my children again. We want to thank you once again. Good night."

Bob and Becky leave the apartment complex.

JERRY THE PROTECTOR

"Bob, we should go check if the shop is open for tomorrow," Becky says. "All I want is to check if the door is unlocked."

Bob turns toward Larry's shop. They arrive at the shop and begin to check the doors. They both meet back at Bob's truck. The radio comes on, and it sounds like Tommy's voice.

"636 to 100."

"Go ahead, 636, this 100."

"Are you at Larry's shop?"

"10-4."

"I am in the shop as well. Could you meet me inside?"

Bob and Becky never notice that Tommy's patrol car is not there. They both walk in and start to look for Tommy. "Tommy!"

Tommy's voice answers, "Over here by the ambulance."

They both walk over to the ambulance and don't see Tommy.

Becky starts to feel nervous. "Bob, are you feeling something?"

"Yes. I feel it too." Bob squeezes the radio's microphone and calls out for Tommy. "100, SO unit 636."

No one answers.

"100. Dispatch."

No one answers.

"Bob, what's going on?" Becky asks. "No one is answering. I don't like this at all."

"Becky, go to my truck and try to use the radio outside," Bob says.

"What about you? Aren't you going outside too?"

"I'll be okay. Just go outside and radio Tommy."

Becky runs outside the shop and calls for Tommy "100 to SO 636."

"100, go ahead. This is 636."

"636, could you go to the apartment complex and pick up Mr. and Mrs. Richards? 100 and myself are at Larry's shop, and we need them over here ASAP!"

"636,100, I am currently busy, but I will swing by their apartment. Could I have the location please?"

Becky realizes that there is a problem. Tommy knew where the apartments were. "100, 636."

"Go ahead, 100."

"Please disregard last traffic. We are not going to need the Richards family, after all."

"10-4."

The lights in the shop begin to flicker. Medic 1's box lights turn on and start to flicker as well. High on the metal rafters, you can see something. It appears to be swirling smoke. It swirls and starts to form a shape. Bob struggles to see what it is. Becky slowly walks over to Bob and is also trying to see what is on the rafters. "What is that, Bob?"

"I can't make it out."

The smoke continues to form into more detail, a shape of a young girl. Her hair is hanging down over her face.

Bob tries to communicate with her and advises her not to move. A voice says, "Please help me. I can't get down!"

Bob begins to climb up toward the rafters. He realizes that he is not going to reach her and tells her, "Look, I can't reach you, but I will call for some help. Okay?"

"You can't reach me, or you won't help me!" The voice changes, and the little girl maneuvers toward Bob.

As she moves, Bob is horrified. The little girl is not a little girl at all. Her hair moves away from her face, and Bob sees a devilish monster moving towards him He tries to climb down but, in his heist, slips and falls to the concrete floor. Bob has broken his leg. The thing continues to climb down toward them, and Becky starts to drag Bob to his feet. Bob clings on to Becky with one arm around her, and they both run toward the shop entry door, but before they can get there, the door slams shut.

Now the thing is on the ground floor and is standing at the other end of the shop area. Becky and Bob stand staring at a monster that has its eyes staring back at them. The figure is slumped over, with its legs bent at the knees. It is leaned to the right, and its claws are touching the concrete floor. It screams at them, displaying its fury. Its mouth opens, and four large caninelike teeth protrude from her jaws. The inside of her mouth is black, and a snakelike red tongue curls out of the way from a mouth full of jagged shaped teeth. Thick saliva clings to the top teeth and dangles toward the bottom jaws. The matted hair appears like large ram horns. Could it be that what they are looking at is the devil himself? It takes a step, and its claws scratch the floor, leaving claw marks in the concrete.

As it walks toward them, it is talking (in Greek). "I αμασηαμεδ οφψου ανδωηατιτις ψου αλλ στανδ φορ. Ψου πριδε ψουρσελρες ας βεινη ηελπερς ανδ ψετ ψου διδ νοτηινγ φορ μψ βροτηερς ανδ σιστερ, ας τηεψ βυρνεδ αλίπε. I ωιλλ μακε ψου παψ φορ ψουρ σελφ-ριγητεους πρξτιξες ανδ ψουρ σελφ σερμινγ αξτς. Ψου τακε πριδε ιν ψουρ αβιλιτψ το σαμε λίρες, βυτ ονλψ δο ιτ ωηεν ιτ βενεφιτς ψου. Ι ωιλλ μακε ψου παψ φορ αλλ τηοσε πεοπλε ψου ξλαιμ το ηαμε ηελπεδ ονλψ το λεαμε ότηερς το διε. Ψου αρε νοτ γοδ, βυτ. Ι ωιλλ σενδ ψου ον ψουρ ωαψ το σεε ηιμ τονιγητ."

(I am ashamed of you and what it is you all stand for. You pride yourselves as being helpers, and yet you did nothing for my brothers and sister as they burned alive. I will make you pay for your self-righteous practices and your self-serving acts. You take pride in your ability to save lives, but only do it when it benefits you. I will make you pay for all those people you claim to have helped only to leave others to die. You are not God, but I will send you on your way to see him tonight.)

Becky yells out, "Lucy, no!"

"So you know my name," Lucy says. "How nice. I know yours as well, Becky."

"Lucy, please understand it wasn't our fault or your parents'. It happened a long time ago."

"Yes, it was your fault, and all others like you. My parents will have their time. Yours is tonight."

It is now four feet from them.

"Lucy, please understand that."

Another voice is heard. "Lucy, my baby, what are you doing?"

It's Lucy's mom. Tommy had been monitoring the radio. He had gone and picked up the Richards and Reverend Michael. Reverend Michael hands Bob a book (*Demon Thesaurus*).

He asks that Bob stay focused on the entity's name. "When the demon says its name, look for the name and tell me what he does and his traits."

Lucy turns toward her mom and leaps in her direction, but is stopped short of clawing into her mother by Jerry.

"You are not hurting anyone else," Jerry says.

"How dare you try to order me?" Lucy says. "They left me, my brothers, and sister to die."

"Lucy, that is not what happened. It was an accident!"

Lucy snaps back, "You were not there. You are just like them."

Other voices are heard. Lucy's brothers and sister approach her.

"Lucy, stop!"

"I will talk to you in a little while," Lucy says. "I need you to go back to bed."

"No, Lucy, you have to stop."

"I am not telling you again. Go to bed *now!*"

The ambulance shakes as if it was in an earthquake. The children scream and run to their parents. Lucy's mom gathers them. "Everything is going to be all right." She tells them that Lucy is just upset. Lucy sees her mother and for a second begins to transform back to normal, but then quickly transforms back to the monster.

"Mother, nothing is going to be all right anymore," Lucy says.

"Lucy, listen to me," Jerry says.

"Okay, Jerry, I am listening." She circles him like a wolf sizing up its prey and showing off her teeth. "Go ahead, Jerry."

"Lucy, please stop."

"Stop or what? You are in no position to threaten me. You have no idea of what I am capable of."

"Lucy, God exists to forgive. He shows us that he does love us very much. If he didn't, we wouldn't be here. If he forgave us, you can forgive them."

Lucy responds in Greek. "Οη Σερρψ ωηετηερ ορ νοτ ηε δοες εχίστ, τηεψ ωιλλ αλλ φινδ ουτ τοδαψ. I ρεμεμβερ ανδ I δο νοτ φοργιFε." (Oh, Jerry, whether or not he does exist, they all will find out today. I remember, and I do not forgive.)

Jerry grabs Lucy in a bear hug. "Give us your name."

Lucy stands and looks up with her mouth open. The building rumbles and shakes.

Jerry asks again, "Give me your name."

Lights start to flash on and off. Light ballasts burst into sparks. Mrs. Richards yells, "What is your name!"

"I am your daughter!" Lucy breaks free from Jerry and throws him against the wall. "So you want to know my name, Mother?"

Throughout the event, someone is mumbling words. Bob looks around and searches the shop to find where it is coming from. It is Reverend Michael reciting a prayer. He recites the prayer meticulously, over and over. He stops only to ask the monster's name. The ambulance rocks and the lights flash faster, on then off.

In an instant, Lucy is in front of Becky. She whispers, in Greek, into Becky's ear, "I αμ τηε δεF iλ ανδ I αμ ηερε το δεFουρ αλλ οφ ψου." (I am the devil, and I am here to devour all of you.)

Lucy slowly places her index finger and claw on Becky's shoulder. Her claw punctures Becky's skin. She slowly advances her long claw further into Becky's shoulder and pins her to the wall.

Becky screams in pain. Bob strikes Lucy with a pipe wrench, and Lucy doesn't even flinch.

Reverend Michael yells, "Give us your name, and prepare yourself for deliverance!"

Lucy again looks up with her mouth open. You can see smokelike vapor spewing from her mouth. She speaks in Greek, "Μψ ναμε iς Λυξψ." (My name is Lucy.) She starts to laugh. The laughter has a deep low tone, and it makes the shop walls vibrate. The sound takes everyone's breath away with the vibration. Mr. Richards stands confused.

"Δον'τ ψου ρεμεμβερ δαδδψ, I αμ ψουρ δαυγητερ." (Don't you remember, Daddy? I am your daughter.)

Jerry grabs her again and pins her to the floor. Mr. Richards yells out, "Please give us your name!"

The tools around the shop begin to fall, and all the glass to all the windows in the shop break into an explosion of glass, sending glass fragments everywhere. The ambulance rocks side to side. Tommy grabs Becky and starts to help her out of the shop. He calls for an ambulance. He returns for Bob.

"Tom, I need to be here," Bob says. "I have to see this."

Jerry then appears to be pulling on something. It is the demon inside of Lucy. He manages to wrap his arms around it. "You are not going to hurt anyone else."

The demon spirit now stands struggling with Jerry. Reverend Michael screams, "Your name, demon?"

Lucy slowly looks up, opens her mouth, and in a low rumbling hellish voice, you can barely hear the name: "Aroooochi!"

Bob searches for the demon's name in the demon thesaurus. "I found it. He is the demon of vengeance."

Reverend Michael orders, "Arochi, demon of vengeance, in the Lord's name, I cast you out. The Lord commands you to leave and let this child sleep. The Lord commands you to your deliverance!"

In an instant, the monster disappears. Jerry is left standing there with nothing in his arms. Lucy turns toward her mother and, in a desperate voice, calls out, "Momma!"

"Lucy!"

Mr. Richards joins them, and all their children embrace each other. Jerry walks over to Bob, who is still on the floor, guarding his broken leg. "Robert, let me help you up."

Bob is astonished at the fact that Jerry is standing in front of him. "Jerry, how is it possible that you are here? I saw you die in the explosion."

"I did, Robert," Jerry says. "But my job here is not done. You will see more of me. I have been granted permission to remain in my present state. It looks like you guys have earned it. I could've asked for a better job. Can you believe it, Bob? I finally made it. Thanks, Robert."

"Thanks for what?" Bob asks.

"For always being there for me and for being a friend." Jerry suddenly hears something, "Got to go, I am needed at an MVA." Jerry disappears in a puff of smoke.

Far at a distance, you can hear the siren of an ambulance approaching. You can see patrol cars arriving and EMS personnel attending to Becky and Bob. Inside the shop, Mr. and Mrs. Richards are kneeling with all their children. Lucy asks why they have to leave.

"Lucy, you are not supposed to be here," Mrs. Richards says.

"But, Mom, I don't want to leave," Lucy says. "I want to stay here with you. We all want to stay here."

"Now, Lucy, we will see you in a little while, but right now, we need you to look after your sister and your brothers. We will see you soon enough. When we do, it will be like old times again. We will finish the play we never got to do."

Lucy holds her brothers' hands and starts to walk away. They say good-bye. As they walk off, they start to disappear in to thin air.

Reverend Michael says a prayer, and they all walk outside the shop.

Bob is left in disbelief. "Reverend, what happened?"

"It seems like Arochi, the demon of vengeance, took advantage of an innocent soul and manipulated the confused child's soul into allowing him to take over. Every demon will always try to hide his name and pretend to be something else. I guess evil never rests. We made it manifest itself by giving us its name, thus exposing himself and any other demon to the deliverer."

"So this was deliverance?" Bob asks. "We made the demon give up his name and, with the help of Jerry, we killed it?"

"It is good that the Lord gave us Jerry to protect us, but remember that Jesus is the deliverer, not us."

GRAND OPENING OF THE NEW STATION 1

"I want to thank everyone for attending the grand opening of our new station," Bob says. "I wanted to thank Mr. White for his complete involvement in the project and, of course, First Frost Bank for funding the project. As the new owner of Orion EMS, together with our staff, we would like to say that we appreciate the support for your public servants. When I took the responsibility of this company, I did so because I felt an overwhelming need to preserve the past. When we regard the past, we make sound decisions.

"I wanted to make sure that everyone that came before us did so to propagate the continuing effort of providing a quality service. Many ambulance companies have come and gone, some bigger than others. Yet we are still here. Is it because we were lucky? I would like to think that it is because of everyone's individual actions. After all, isn't that what defines any company, the experiences and abilities of its employees? We must believe that we are here as part of something bigger and let that be sufficient enough to endure this heartache and many more to come. I do not want to encourage anyone to be a martyr, but be more like Atlas, the embodiment of endurance and strength. Thank you.

"I would like to have a moment of silence and a traditional sounding of our siren for Jerry Sanchez, a paramedic, a very dear friend and brother. To Jerry Sanchez, may God bless you and hold you close. We will all miss you very much."

There was a moment of silence, and the serene is sounded. Jerry Sanchez's badge number is called out for the last time over the radio: "Dispatch to 201. Dispatch to 201. 10-4—201 God speed."

"Thank you very much for attending," Bob says. "Please feel free to enjoy the festivities, and don't eat too many hot dogs. We don't want to transport anybody to the hospital."

"Hey, Bob, do we start the station tours yet?" Becky asks.

Bob smiles. "Becky, do you really need me to get involved with that? And for your information, you can address me as Mr. Matt. Please."

Just then a tone is heard. "KB 1437. Orion EMS, we have a request for an ambulance for a possible injured leg."

Frank looks at Becky.

"Don't look at me," Becky says. "Go find your partner and take off."

"Yes, ma'am, supe."

Frank and his partner jump into the front seats of the ambulance. Frank turns the ignition key, and the unit starts like a match. All the LED emergency lights turn on. The ambulance comes alive. It creeps forward, and you can hear the sound of a siren coming out of two 100-watt speakers. The sound drowns out the roar of a powerful diesel engine. You hear two blasts of a train sound emanate from the air horns.

As it pulls forward, you can see a unit number on both front fenders, "Medic One." Right underneath the number, you also see "In Memory of Jerry Sanchez." The ambulance bolts forward and on its way to the emergency call.

Frank Chavez holds the steering wheel with both hands and stares out the front windshield with both eyes wide open. His partner, Victor Ortiz, holds on to the dashboard with his left hand and grabs the door armrest with his right. Victor is a rookie, and totally acts the part. He notices something in the rear box and gets startled. "Did you see that, in the back?"

Frank smiles. "Yep, it's Jerry. He is here to take care of us. Don't worry, everything is gonna be alright, Jerry is on the call."

WHAT IS THE NAME

In a dark room an alarm is screaming wake up. You know that annoying buzzing sound. The sound that rattles your brain. It screams at you to wake up and makes you regret, you even set it at the crazy time. Samantha moans as she reaches over from her side of the bed and over to her husband side, to turn it off. In a darkened kitchen William is pouring coffee in a tumbler as he scrolls through his cell phone and his investment apps.

"Dammit!!!" "I can never get this right," He opens his refrigerator grabs some bologna, mayo and mustard. He opens the loaf of bread bag and discovers that his down to his last couple of slices. He reaches in and pulls out three pieces of semi-square bread and one oddly shaped bread loaf end. He smiles and concedes that at least he can call it a sandwich. He walks outside and jumps into his compact car, huffs and puffs as he sits in the driver seat. His place of work is not that far away, but must hurry before he catches all the red lights. Looks like he is gonna see red lights all morning. The car starts right up and revs' up. Of course, he drives a four cylinder coupe. Its slow, but William is okay with that. He backs up and takes off to work.

As he drives in to his works parking lot, he notices something strange sitting in the "Recent Arrival" section of the salvage yard. He opens the front door and is greeted by Sara Ericks the office manager and over all boss lady. Good morning sir she politely says to William. "Good Morning! Hey Sara what is up with the perfect looking ambulance in the new arrivals section. She cringes at the idea that junked vehicles would be anything else than a burnt pile of rusted metal and aluminum. She has seen William Benson of Benson Steel be frugal on far too many items. Smiles and answers, "Don't know sir." "Can you check if we have all the proper paperwork for that ambulance" "I did sir, spoke with a gentleman name Bob Matt and confirmed. He definitely did not want it and asked that we crush it as soon as we could." "One more thing Sara, when you get a chance can you get Mr. Phillips and Mr. Jacobson on the phone, they might be interested in the ambulance?" "You mean to sell them the ambulance?" "Yeap!!" A few minutes later the office phone begins to ring. "Mr. Benson, You have conference call. Mr. Phillips and Mr. Jacobson are on line one."

Afternoon Gentleman, I have a great deal on a wonderful looking Ambulance. I am not too sure but I think its a Type 1 ambulance. Its got a diesel engine with all the bells and whistles. Also has air horns, its just a wonderful looking unit." "William, you have an ambulance in your salvage yard? You serious?" "Yes sir, I am looking at as we speak." "How much are you asking for it?" "Hey, judging by the looks of it, I think its worth approximately $110,000. You all can have it for $80,000." "No way William, that you have that kind of an ambulance in your yard and for sale." "Okay, if you want to see it, drive down here and look at it for yourselves." "We can use another ambulance in our fleet." "Waiting for you guys here."

"Sara, get the guys to start cleaning up the ambulance its gonna be sold" "No way" Sara shouts in disbelief. "That ambulance is a burnt up pile of junk." "What do you mean? Come here, I can see it with the cameras. Take a look" As Sara goes around William's desk and stares at the screen. Astonished she cant believe it. "William, gets on the radio and relays to his yard men to prepare the ambulance for sale. One of the Yardmen jumps in the driver seat cranks it on and it starts up like a match. It idles down to a faint whistle of the turbo charger. "Wow!" He puts in gear and the unit creeps forward. and there on the side fender just behind the fender well, you see a name painted on it. You cant see it at first. You have to get closer and closer, its becoming clearer. What is the name?

"LUCY"